D0521681

A6.

Cobra Threat

Books by Sigmund Brouwer

SPORTS MYSTERY SERIES

#1 *Maverick Mania*

#2 *Tiger Heat*

#3 *Cobra Threat* (available 8/98)

#4 *Titan Clash* (available 10/98)

LIGHTNING ON ICE SERIES

#1 *Rebel Glory*

#2 *All-Star Pride*

#3 *Thunderbird Spirit*

#4 *Winter Hawk Star*

#5 *Blazer Drive*

#6 *Chief Honor*

SHORT CUTS SERIES

#1 *Snowboarding to the Extreme . . . Rippin'*

#2 *Mountain Biking to the Extreme . . . Cliff Dive*

#3 *Skydiving to the Extreme . . . 'Chute Roll*

#4 *Scuba Diving to the Extreme . . . Off the Wall*

CYBERQUEST SERIES

#1 *Pharaoh's Tomb*

#2 *Knight's Honor*

#3 *Pirate's Cross*

#4 *Outlaw's Gold*

#5 *Soldier's Aim*

#6 *Galilee Man*

THE ACCIDENTAL DETECTIVES MYSTERY SERIES

WINDS OF LIGHT MEDIEVAL ADVENTURES

SPORTS MYSTERY SERIES

Cobra Threat

SIGMUND BROUWER

Thomas Nelson, Inc.

Nashville

COBRA THREAT

Published in Nashville, Tennessee, by Tommy Nelson™,
a division of Thomas Nelson, Inc.

Executive Editor: Laura Minchew; Managing Editor: Beverly Phillips.
Cover Photograph: NSP/PP

Library of Congress Cataloging-in-Publication Data

Brouwer, Sigmund, 1959–
    Cobra threat.
       p. cm.—(Sigmund Brouwer's sports mystery series)
    Summary: After discovering tainted water in the creek near his
grandmother's cabin in the Kentucky hills, senior Roy Linden slowly
uncovers a connection between his high school team's new star
quarterback, his own football future, and the source of the
pollution.
    ISBN 0-8499-5815-6
    [1. Orphans—Fiction. 2. Football—Fiction. 3. Stuttering—
Fiction. 4. Pollution—Fiction. 5. Kentucky—Fiction. 6. Mystery
and detective stories.] I. Title. II. Series: Brouwer, Sigmund,
1959–   Sports mystery series.
PZ7.B79984Co   1998
[Fic]—dc21

                                                    98-23259
                                                       CIP
                                                        AC

Printed in the United States of America
98 99 00 01 02 03 DHC 9 8 7 6 5 4 3 2 1

To Debra and Tina and Leanne
at the Young Writers Institute

One

When I left the science lab after school on Friday, I had two problems. The first was what I had discovered in the lab. The second was that spending extra time there had made me fifteen minutes late for football practice.

Because of that, I didn't reach the locker room until most of my teammates on the Johnstown Striking Cobras had already changed and gone into the gym. And because I was the last one out of the locker room, I was the only one to see Glenn Pitt, our assistant coach, grab the wrong can of Pepsi. He had mistakenly reached for one filled with the dark brown juice of chewing tobacco spit.

But I should probably back up a bit to tell the whole story.

When I walked out of the locker room, the high school gym was filled with guys in sweats sprinting back and forth. Between me and those guys, our two football coaches stood in front of a table covered with papers of team plays. The men stood with their backs toward me. Each coach carried a clipboard. Each had a stopwatch. Each was timing the short sprints of the guys in sweats and making notes on his clipboard.

Normally, we practiced outside on the football field. But today rain pounded so hard that the skylights of the gym rumbled like gravel in a clothes dryer. Not even our coaches—who thought cold and pain and torture were the keys to turning us into men—had the heart to make us churn through the cold mud in this rain.

Or maybe they just wanted a better, upclose look at all the players—this was the last afternoon of tryouts. Old Coach Donaldson wore glasses so thick that they made his eyes look like little brown peas floating somewhere deep in an aquarium. If rain streaked those glasses, he became as blind as he was already deaf.

But our assistant coach, Glenn Pitt, had perfect eyesight and hearing. He was young, just out of college. He had won bodybuilding competitions, and with his short, dark hair and bullet-shaped skull, he could have been a poster boy for the marines.

Coach Pitt was the complete opposite of Coach Donaldson, who some people joked had started coaching high school football teams before college teams were even invented. Coach Donaldson was certainly no marine. He looked like a giant pear, with a gray bowling ball-shaped head plunked on top and stiltlike legs sticking out below.

I watched them for a few seconds, wishing I could somehow sneak past Coach Pitt's eagle eyes. Once he noticed I was late, he would yell at me. He liked to yell, especially at me, because I had a hard time defending myself.

Worse, I would have to tell him why I was late on the last day of tryouts. I knew he'd yell even louder when he learned I'd put science ahead of football. But that part I could handle. The part I couldn't handle was saying the words *Pitt* and *science*. Which would give Coach Pitt even more opportunity to yell at me.

So I waited, hoping some miracle would happen to let me get past him unnoticed.

The squeaks of running shoes on the gym floor mixed with grunts and shouts. If only I were already out there with the other guys. . . .

Clipboard in his left hand, Coach Donaldson used his right hand to bring a Pepsi can to his mouth. He squirted a stream of tobacco juice into the can. He almost always had a golf ball-sized wad of chewing tobacco bulging his cheek out. Outdoors, he just fired tobacco juice onto the grass, and if a player was unlucky enough to slide into it during a tackle, it stuck and smeared across his jersey like grasshopper guts. Here, indoors, Coach Donaldson had no choice but to spit into a Pepsi can, which was only slightly less gross; it was hard to aim into the can, and much of the juice dribbled down his chin.

A football came wobbling across the floor toward Coach Donaldson's feet. Jim Schenley, our quarterback, had been warming up in the back of the gym and—no surprise—he had fired the ball way over the head of his receiver.

Coach Donaldson set his Pepsi can on the table behind him and grabbed the football. It probably broke his heart that the best quarterback he could find for this team had an arm with the accuracy of a broken watch.

Coach Pitt, who had focused his attention on the sprinters directly in front of him, did not notice Coach Donaldson pick up the ball. Or put down his Pepsi can on the table behind him. Trouble was, Coach Pitt had left his own can of Pepsi sitting on the table.

As Coach Donaldson wandered away with the football to talk to Schenley, Coach Pitt absently reached behind him for his Pepsi. His eyes and attention stayed on the sprinters, however, and his fingers closed around Coach Donaldson's can instead of his own.

He began to lift the can to his mouth, but stopped halfway. A couple of players were laughing at a joke on the other side of the gym.

"Hey, Martins, Taylor," Coach Pitt yelled, "this is practice. Not a tea party. Drop and give me twenty-five push-ups!"

Coach Pitt grinned in mean delight and loudly counted off the push-ups as Martins and Taylor began. Everyone stopped and stared, glad Coach Pitt was picking on someone else.

Me? I stared at the Pepsi can in Coach Pitt's hand.

There was my miracle.

His Pepsi must have been close enough to empty that it felt about the same weight as Coach Donaldson's can of tobacco spit. All I had to do was keep my mouth shut, and Coach Pitt would take a swig of that horrible brown juice. He'd be so busy gagging that I'd have the perfect chance to get out there among the players without being noticed.

If that wasn't enough reason to keep my mouth shut, there was also the fact that Coach Pitt laughed at me every time I spoke and called me a "b-b-baby."

I was really tempted to stay where I was and watch.

But I could picture Gram in her rocking chair on the porch, smiling sadly at me for repaying bad with bad.

So I stepped forward.

I tried to call out. In my mind, I heard my words perfectly: *No! Coach Pitt, don't drink from that Pepsi can.*

But as always, my throat tightened when I tried to speak. It was worse around Coach Pitt because he made me extra nervous.

So what came out was a low whistling squeal that Coach could not hear above his own loud counting.

I had no choice but to tap him on the shoulder.

He spun around.

"What!" he yelled, angry that someone had interrupted him.

His eyes got big when he saw who'd had the nerve to stop him.

"L-l-linden," he said, his lips curling in joy at the chance to hassle me.

He turned away from me for a second and shouted to the rest of the team.

"Listen up guys, L-l-linden is about to explain to everyone why he's l-l-late."

The last squeaks of rubber soles against the gym floor stopped. As did all other noise. Most of the guys hate it when Coach teases me, almost as much as I do. But few would dare to make noise now and bring his wrath on themselves. It was just me and the huge echoing space of the gym—with the entire team listening.

My throat got tighter. I hate attention. The great thing about football is that when you play, you can hide your face inside a helmet. And you don't have to talk.

With all eyes on me, I again heard my words clearly in my head. *Coach Pitt, you grabbed the wrong Pepsi can.*

"C-c-c-c-c . . ." I almost stomped my foot in the effort to get it out. "C-c-c-c-c . . ."

I stopped. With everyone staring, I couldn't force the word out.

"Coach," he said, grinning with delight. "Spit it out, Mr. B-baby Talk. *Coach.*"

"C-c-c-c-c-oach P-p-p-p . . ."

"Coach Pitt . . ." he said, nodding. I knew some of the guys on the team were squirming for me. Just like most people did whenever I had to talk to them.

"K-k-keep g-g-oing," he said. "You c-c-can do it."

His eyes gleamed. I was his favorite target.

"Y-y-you gr-gr-gr-gr-gr-gr . . ." I said. Most of the time, when I get stuck on a word, I search for a different one that's easier to say. But with his big mean grin on me, I felt frozen like a frog in a flashlight beam.

He laughed again. And waved me quiet.

"We d-d-d-on't have all n-n-night," Coach Pitt said loudly so everyone could hear. "Hit the floor and g-g-give me a hundred p-p-p-ush-ups."

I pointed at the can of Pepsi in his hand.

"The wr-r-r-r . . ."

"Down, Linden!" he yelled with sudden rage. "Now!"

With a nasty grin of triumph, he tilted his head back and sucked in a big gulp from the Pepsi can. And instead of cool, refreshing Pepsi, he swallowed warm horrible slime.

I saw it first in his eyes. They instantly popped wide in disbelief.

He dropped the can and clutched his throat.

"L-like I was tr-rying to say," I explained. Words came out easier now that I didn't feel the pressure. "You gr-r-rabbed the c-can with t-t-obacco juice."

His eyes crossed.

He slapped both hands across his mouth.

He dashed past me to the locker room.

Even before the doors banged shut, we all heard it.

Loud, anguished retching as he threw up.

He didn't make it back to practice. And I never did my hundred push-ups.

Two

That night, as I usually do on Fridays, I set my alarm to get up early, so I could visit my grandmother Saturday morning.

Unfortunately, I had bad news to deliver.

Any other time, visiting her was something I looked forward to, partly because she lives back in the hills. I love any excuse to drive my Chevy truck along those lonely winding roads shaded by trees. The main reason I enjoy visiting her, though, is there is no other person in the world who means more to me. My parents died in a car crash when I was three, and I grew up in town with my aunt and uncle. Their youngest son is ten years older than me, so it's never really seemed like I have a close family.

Except for Gram. I've spent most of my summers with her, and she's taught me a lot about the land and nature, taking me into the woods and showing me flowers and roots and how they can be used for medicine. Pointing out the different birds and their habits. Showing me how to sneak up on deer. That's where I feel the most comfortable—among the trees and grass. Where a person doesn't have to talk.

When my alarm went off at 7:00 A.M., I dressed in jeans and a sweatshirt without showering. In the kitchen, I grabbed an apple to eat during my drive. I wanted to save my appetite for Gram's country breakfast. No one else was up, and I left quietly after leaving a note for my aunt and uncle.

My truck started at the first turn of the key. I let it purr for a few minutes. It's an old truck, but I work on it plenty and keep it in good running condition.

The sky was a cloudless blue, but water from last night's rain spotted the windshield. I let the wipers run and adjusted the defroster so my breathing wouldn't fog the inside of the windows. I put the truck into gear and pulled away from Uncle Jeb's house, a white two-story building in a row of white two-story buildings on a street lined with old, tall trees.

Although I was a high school senior and I had lived in this house since I was three, I never thought of it as home. It was always "Uncle Jeb's house." Maybe it was because Uncle Jeb and Aunt Marlene treated me so politely, as if they were afraid I would break in two if they hugged me or raised their voices or did any of the rough-and-tumble things parents did when they treated their kids like kids. Or maybe it was just too awkward for them to talk to me. I had so much trouble getting my words out, they always seemed to be looking away out of embarrassment. Either way—with their kids grown up and gone, and just us three in the house—living with them has been quiet. Most of my memories of the house are about how it squeaks and creaks as we move through it ever so politely.

I turned the corner, and Uncle Jeb's house disappeared from my rearview mirror.

It didn't take me long to get out of town. Not because we live close to the edge of town, but because there isn't much town. It only has one high school and doesn't even have a McDonald's or a Burger King. This is just a small forgotten place stuck back in the hills of southeast Kentucky.

I drove down Main Street, past the old courthouse. On the seat beside me was a mini-recorder, the kind people use to dictate notes. I grabbed it and pressed the record button.

"I am dead, Horatio," I said into the microphone. "Wretched queen, good-bye! You that look pale and tremble at this chance, that are but mutes or audience to this act. Had I but time, I could tell you. But let it be. Horatio, I am dead."

I snapped the record button off, rewound the tape, and played it back. My words were getting clearer.

Saying lines I had memorized from Shakespeare's play *Hamlet* was one way I worked on conquering my stutter. No one had told me it would help, but I figured it couldn't hurt. I liked the sound of the words the way Shakespeare wrote them. And people have used worse methods to try to cure their stuttering.

There was this Greek named Demosthenes who became a famous speaker even though he stuttered. He practiced speaking with pebbles under his tongue, and he stood at the sea and shouted above the roar of the waves. To make his lungs more powerful, he strapped a weight to his chest and recited things as he ran up hills.

Thinking about famous people who stuttered and got over it always made me feel better. The guy who wrote *Alice in Wonderland*—Lewis Carroll—stuttered. So did a famous British prime minister, Winston Churchill. And Marilyn Monroe.

I've always told myself that if they could get past their stutter, so could I.

"Now cracks a noble heart," I said into the tape recorder. This was Horatio, talking back to Hamlet after Hamlet had been hit by a sword tipped with poison. Shakespeare wrote some good action stories. "Good night, sweet prince, and flights of angels sing thee to rest!"

I practiced more as I drove down Main Street. When I reached the railroad tracks, I turned and followed them along the river. I reached for the apple, crunching on it to knock the edge off my hunger.

Along this road, I passed the Johns Corporation warehouses. I passed the Johns Corporation trucking center. I passed the Johns Corporation headquarters. I passed almost a mile's worth of Johns Corporation civic pride. All of the buildings were set behind beautifully landscaped lawns with ponds and flower beds.

The Johns Corporation had begun as a coal mine at the turn of the century and had expanded ever since. Most people in town worked for the Johns Corporation in one way or another. It didn't take a rocket scientist to figure out why this little town in the valley was called Johnstown.

And that made the news I had for Gram even worse. I was worried that my bad news was somehow connected with all those nice buildings that overlooked those perfectly landscaped lawns. Just like I was worried the Johns Corporation had made it necessary for me to need the empty jars rolling around on the floor of my truck.

Twenty minutes later, as I parked near Gram's cabin, I had rehearsed what I needed to explain to her.

Three

From where I parked the truck beneath an elm tree, I could see Gram. She sat in her rocker on the front porch, reading from her Bible.

In some ways, Gram was what you'd expect a granny to look like. She favored dark dresses. Her white hair was piled in a bun. She had tiny glasses perched on her nose. Her cheeks looked like wrinkly dried apples.

But in other ways, she wasn't what you'd expect at all. Although in her eighties, she could still dance and giggle like a teenager. Her eyes were a deep, clear blue that any movie star would envy. Her voice, thick with a backwoods drawl, was soft and quiet and, especially when she was angry, hinted of great power.

I walked across grass wet with dew up the slight hill to her cabin. It wasn't much more than a bedroom and kitchen, with a small living room warmed by a stone fireplace. The outside walls of the cabin had weathered to a soft gray over the years; the roof was dull tin. But not one piece of lumber sagged. Old as the cabin was, it had been built sturdy.

Gram looked up and smiled at my approach. The morning's first sun warmed the front porch of the cabin, and the shadow from Gram's head fell across the Bible on her lap.

"He was good, that Jesus," she said as a hello to me.

"Yes, ma'am," I said. I didn't stutter as much around Gram. While there is plenty that doctors don't know about stuttering, they do know it seems to happen when we tighten our vocal cords and they lock up. Part of why we tighten, though, is because we're afraid we're going to stutter. And the more we are afraid, the more we stutter. So the problem just keeps getting worse. Around Gram, though, I'm less afraid of stuttering because I know she doesn't care if I do, and because I'm less afraid, I stutter less.

Gram took off her reading glasses, folded them, and set them on her lap beside the Bible. "Even folks who don't believe in his miracles will agree he was a great teacher, that thousands followed him and hung on his every word. But did he charge admission? Did he ask for a collection plate? No sir."

She sighed and shook her head. "Just heard on the radio about another television preacher caught doing wrong. Them's the ones so caught up in wordly riches they forget the teachings—how a soul is worth so much more than anything the world can give them."

She sighed again. "So when I get discouraged hearing about those who use Jesus and his teachings badly, I just go right back to the source." She patted her Bible. "Helps me remember all over again how good God is. And my faith don't get tarnished none."

"Yes, ma'am," I said. Sometimes I disagree with her, just for the fun of getting her all worked up and excited. This morning, however, I didn't have the heart for it. I had too much else on my mind.

She patted the Bible again. "This does give me comfort as I gets closer and closer to the pearly gates."

"Yes, ma'am," I said.

Gram leaned forward and peered at me. "Don't 'yes ma'am' me like I'm some child you want to keep happy. You should be telling me them pearly gates is still a long ways off. And furthermore, you and me have had enough talks. You should be chastising me for calling them the pearly gates. As if heaven's such a small place that gates can contain it."

"Yes, ma'am," I said, finally grinning.

"That's better," she said. "You looked like you'd just left a funeral."

She pointed at the rocking chair beside her. "Set yourself down," she said, "and tell me what's eating you. And I know it ain't football."

I set myself down. "Ma'am?"

"There's no way you didn't make the team," she said. "Not my Roy Linden, the boy who's fast enough to slap a deer's rump."

"Gram, it was j-just once, and I wish you w-w-wouldn't keep on with that story."

"You cain't deny it. And folks around here have seen you run. They know it's the truth."

Gram had been with me that afternoon. Back when I was fourteen. I had been standing at the edge of a clearing, downwind from the yearling doe so it couldn't catch my smell, with enough of a wind that it couldn't hear me move softly through the deep grass. I'd gotten close enough to see its eyelashes. I'd burst up from the grass, not even sure myself why I was doing it. But I'd gotten enough of a jump to swat the doe's hind end as it started to run from me.

"'Course," Gram said, "legs like yours don't do a team no good without someone who's got an arm to take advantage of it. Anyone else show up for quarterback besides that pitiful boy of the Schenleys'?"

"No, ma'am." Usually this was how we spent our time. She talked a lot to spare me the effort.

Gram shook her head in disgust. "That boy's arm don't have the power to throw a football through a wet paper towel. It's a shame. A real shame. You're probably the best-kept secret playing football in Kentucky 'cause there's no one to get you the ball."

"Gram, you're s-saying that because you're s-supposed to."

"No," she said, "I'm saying it because I could go to my grave a happy woman knowing that those fleet legs of yours got you a scholarship to college. Be the best chance you have of making something of yourself

16

and leaving this coal town. And it ain't going to happen with a quarterback like that Schenley boy. Your team's got to win some games before any scouts will make the visit to Johnstown."

We sat quietly for a few minutes, each of us rocking as we enjoyed the sunshine and the trees and the view of the valley beyond the trees. In a few weeks, when autumn frost struck, the vivid colors in the trees as their leaves turned would make the woods look like a storybook picture.

Finally, Gram sighed to break our silence. "Is it about the water? Is that why you come up here so glum?"

Gram always could read my mind. She knew what was weighing me down.

"Yes, ma'am. It is."

And I began to tell her my bad news.

Four

Although I stutter less around Gram than around others, talking still doesn't come easily. And every once in a while I get mad at myself because the words I hear in my head don't come out as fast as I can think them.

So it took me a while to tell her what I had discovered in the science lab just before football practice.

In the last couple of months, Gram has found several dead birds near her cabin. Not dead like killed by foxes dead, with piles of feathers scattered around a bush. These birds looked more like they had flown into a window. Tiny perfect bundles of color that would never sing again. Gram's found them in her garden, under her apple trees, and even in the creek, trapped against roots and fallen branches by the force of the current.

Gram doesn't believe in using pesticides on her apple trees or in her garden. She started to wonder if something in the water was killing those birds. There is a spring-fed creek—Gram calls it a crick—that runs past her cabin, which is perched halfway up a hill and overlooks the hollow—she calls it a holler. Near the cabin, the creek widens to make a small pond then narrows again and flows into the bottom of the hollow to join a small river.

Gram started to worry when she hadn't seen a frog or a turtle in the pond in a while.

She had been right to worry about the water.

In the science lab, I'd looked at two water samples through a microscope. The first sample came from a creek in a valley on the other side of the hill. The second sample came from the pond near Gram's cabin.

In the first sample I saw what I had expected to from all the things I had learned in biology. There were dozens of little wriggly things, so small they were invisible without the microscope. As my biology teacher had explained, they were the beginning of the food chain. Roughly speaking, they were food for tiny bugs, which became food for bigger bugs, and the bigger bugs became food for birds and so on up the line.

The first sample, then, was normal.

In the sample from Gram's pond, though, I saw hardly anything through the microscope. It looked like tap water: Nothing wriggled in it.

"Chemicals," Gram grimly announced when I told her what I'd seen. "It's chemicals what's killed the tiny wrigglers. And chemicals what's killed the birds. How did chemicals get in my crick?"

I shook my head. "Th-that's what I've been trying to

figure out, Gram. All I can th-think of is the Johns Corporation and the c-coal mining. B-but I've looked at the county m-m-maps. Th-he closest m-mine shaft is a few miles south of here, clear over Lookout H-h-hill."

"Chemicals," she repeated with conviction. "Mark my words. Something unnatural. Can you do some sort of special test on the water to find out what's in it?"

"I can give a s-sample to the c-county health dep-dep-dep-dep . . ."—I gave up on the word *department* and did what I sometimes do: found another word—"officials."

Gram nodded briskly. "Do that then."

I'd been worrying about something ever since I'd looked at the pond water sample. "Wh-what about y-your w-w-well?" I asked. Being nervous about her drinking water was hurting my words. "Wh-what if the w-water is . . ."

"It's not," she said firmly. "That well draws from a hundred feet down. Purest water a body can drink. Besides, it'll take more than bad water to put me in a cold grave."

I didn't disagree. Still, when Gram went inside to fix breakfast, I went back down to my truck. I had brought the empty jars that had rolled around on the floor for a reason. After breakfast, I would fill them with water samples from different places along the creek, upstream and downstream, to see where the bad water began and how far it went.

I took one of those empty jars and wrote on the label

in red ink: WATER SAMPLE FROM CLAIRE LINDEN'S WELL. COLLECTED ON SEPTEMBER 10.

I went to her well and pumped until cold water flowed to fill the jar. I tightened the lid and stashed the jar in my truck.

It would go with all the other samples to the county health department.

Tough as Gram was, I couldn't help but think of those little birds—so stiff and silent and much too dead. And I couldn't help but think how horrible it would be for the same thing to happen to Gram.

# Five

In the locker room the following Friday night, the entire team gathered to listen as Coach Pitt gave us a pep talk on winning the game. Coach Donaldson had gone outside to talk to the referees.

Coach Pitt repeated the same old rah-rah things we'd heard dozens of times before, and I began to think about the water in Gram's creek. I wasn't smart enough to keep my eyes on Coach Pitt, though, and without warning, he began to yell at me.

"Linden! Pay attention! Don't you care about this game?"

I nodded.

"Speak to me, Linden. Be a man!"

"I c-c-c-c . . ." I felt my face turning red.

"C-c-come on, L-l-linden," Coach Pitt began with a sneer. "T-t-talk."

Flustered, I couldn't get a word out. I felt tears of frustration threaten to start.

Then a clear voice came from somewhere in the middle of the team. "T-t-t-tobacco j-j-j-juice!"

Everyone busted up.

"Who said that?" Coach Pitt yelled. He hated being laughed at. Maybe that's why he picked on others. When no one answered, he repeated, "Who said that?!"

Again no answer. But a lot of snorting laughter.

"All right," Coach Pitt said. The anger in his voice caused us to quiet down. "Linden, give me one hundred push-ups. Now."

I took a deep breath, remembering what Gram had told me. Weak people picked on others, just to make themselves feel better. This was Coach Pitt's problem. Not mine. But as I dropped to the ground, to my surprise, so did a bunch of my teammates. They began to do push-ups with me. In a few seconds, everyone had joined us.

Coach Pitt was speechless.

But Coach Donaldson wasn't. He walked in and found his whole team doing push-ups.

"Pitt," he said. "It's tough enough for these kids to win games. Do you have to tire them out before the game even begins?"

Coach Donaldson told us to get up and then sent us out to the field.

I guessed Pitt wouldn't bother me again soon.

I stood in the backfield, waiting. The night was warm, and big moths darted around the lights above the field. A huge crowd had gathered for our first home game of the season.

In seconds, we would start the first play. With me as part of the suicide squad.

That's what they called those of us who played on the kick return team. Even though I'm a receiver, our high school is so small that a lot of us have to play more than one position.

But why call us the suicide squad?

Think of it this way. The kickoff is one of the few times when the opposing team has a chance to gain sixty yards' worth of steam before trying to mow down the ball carrier.

And, against tonight's team, the Penhold Panthers, that sixty yards' worth of full speed could be painful. Because, of all the teams in the league, these guys were among the biggest.

Add up all the weight of the football equipment: helmet, shoulder pads, hip pads, thigh pads, knee pads, elbow pads, rib pads. It's about fifty or sixty pounds—more on a rainy day when the padding soaks up water.

Now put that sixty pounds on guys who already weigh close to two hundred pounds—like most of the defensive tackles on the Panthers. It turns them into tanks.

The ref dropped his arm to start the game. Their kicker ran forward and leaned into the ball. It sailed so high, I lost it briefly against the glare of the setting sun.

Then, there it was. Tumbling down from the sky like a shot goose. My side of the field.

I looked ahead briefly and saw that our guards were forming a wedge to protect me.

I backed up several steps, then timed it so that as I ran forward again, I caught the ball in the center of my stomach. I wanted my feet in motion when I got the ball.

As I connected, the Panthers began hitting our line. Above the screaming of the crowd, I heard the popping sounds of helmets and shoulder pads meeting at full speed and the grunts of bodies colliding.

Within seconds, the Panthers had destroyed the wedge and were swarming toward me.

It's a lot easier to turn at full speed than from a standstill. The key to outmaneuvering your opponent is to keep your feet moving. Which I did.

The first Panther dived toward me, but I was able to cut left and jump over two fallen players. His hands plucked at my jersey as I slipped loose.

I took another quick look up the field. I could see a gap to my right. I blasted toward it, hearing more grunts as tacklers missed me and connected with the ground.

A shoulder fake to the left, and a duck to the right put me past another two players.

And just like that, there were only three men between me and the end zone.

I kicked into full speed, with two tackles angling toward me. I outran one of them. The other got a hand on my shoulder, but I shook him off and he lost his balance. As he fell, he grabbed at my leg. I stumbled, nearly fell, but recovered.

Only one tackle ahead. Others chasing me from behind.

I headed back to my left, to the most open part of the field.

Maybe I couldn't talk well, but I did know how to run. Getting to a place where I could use full speed would be to my advantage.

It was.

The last tackle made a dive at me and fell short.

I heard two tackles chasing me hard from behind. But with no one left between me and the end zone, it became a foot race. I wasn't going to lose.

I put my head down and stretched hard, gaining five yards, then seven yards, then ten yards on my pursuers. By the time I crossed the goal line, I had a fifteen-yard lead.

I lifted my arms high as the crowd roared its delight.

First game. First play. First touchdown.

It felt great.

I dropped the ball and stood with my hands on my knees, gasping for breath as the rest of my team caught up to me.

The extra point was good, and we were up 7–0.

Our joy lasted for about five minutes.

That's how long it took for the Panthers to work the ball back to our end and score an answering touchdown. And the point after.

Seven to seven.

On the next kickoff, the Panthers kept the ball away from me and forced us to begin a drive on our own ten-yard line.

On our first play, Schenley, our quarterback, threw up a marshmallow that their safety picked out of the air.

I tackled him as he tried to run the ball in for a touchdown. But we'd lost the possession.

Two plays later, the Panther quarterback ran the ball in himself. Just like that, we were down 13–7. With the point after, 14–7.

It only got worse from there. Schenley was intercepted another dozen times—probably some sort of pitiful record. We lost 49–7.

First game. First loss. And with Schenley as our only quarterback, it looked like it wouldn't be our last.

 *Six*

Monday afternoon, I stood waiting all alone at the front desk of the county offices, a low, square brick building on Main Street. As I looked around, I realized the inside was as boring to look at as the outside.

Beyond the front desk was a hallway lined with tiny windowless offices. I could see into the nearest offices; each held a small desk and lots of paper clutter. The walls all around me were dull white with no pictures. The air was stale and smelled a little like old sweat.

I waited a while longer. I finally cleared my throat, hoping someone would come out of one of the offices down the hallway.

A few minutes later, I heard rustling, the sound of nylon against nylon. A skinny woman in a bright red dress came out of a carpeted office and clicked down the hallway toward me in high heels.

"Yes?" she asked. She stopped behind the front desk, looking not at me but at her nails, shiny and as red as her dress. Huge fake eyelashes fluttered with every movement of her eyelids.

"I w-w-was here l-l-last M-monday," I said. "W-w-w-with w-water s-samples."

I could tell she was getting impatient with my slow words. That just made it worse for me.

"I l-l-left th-th-them w-w-w—"

"Yeah," she said, cutting me off. "With Fred. Our health inspector."

That was one advantage, I guess, about stuttering. People remembered you.

She half turned and bellowed back down the hallway. "Fred! Drag those lazy bones of yours out of the coffee room. You've got a visitor!"

She went back to studying her fingernails. She saw a bit of lint and blew it off, then buffed her nails against the shoulder of her dress.

Fred finally appeared. I knew what he looked like, of course, from the week before. An older man about my height, with thinning brown hair, tired eyes, and a sagging face. He was wearing the same brown suit and same stained tie he'd had on the last time I'd seen him.

"Oh," he said when he saw me. Like I was a tax collector.

Oh? No big grin and handshake? Last Monday he had greeted me like a long-lost buddy. A Cobra fan, he'd recognized me and told me how much he was looking forward to watching us this season. In a small town like ours, high school football was a big deal. Almost everybody followed the team closely. Had I played so badly against the Panthers that he didn't even want to talk football?

"Hmmmm, hello," I said. "I'm here about the w-w-water samples."

Sometimes, when I know what I want to say ahead of time, I can practice the words in my mind. By humming a bit, I can loosen up my throat. That makes it easier to get the words started.

"Yeah," he said. "The water samples."

I waited. I do that as often as I can instead of asking obvious questions. Like, in this case, were the tests done like he had promised?

"I got good news," he said. "There's not a thing wrong with the water you brought me."

That surprised me so much I blurted out without thinking, "Th-that can't b-b-be."

"Are you calling me a liar?" he asked, getting defensive. "I tell you, everything tested so pure that I'd drink it myself."

"B-b-but under th-the m-m-m-m . . ." I had said the wrong thing and made him mad. Which made me so nervous I was forgetting to concentrate on how to shape the words with my mouth.

"Under th-th-the m-m-m-m . . ." I stopped again. I couldn't think of another word for *microscope*.

I pulled a small notepad and pen from the back pocket of my jeans. I wrote as quickly as I could:

Under the microscope, it looked different from other pond-water samples.

While the skinny woman in the red dress snickered at me, I handed the note to Fred. I hated having to use the notebook, but I always keep it handy for times like this. Unfortunately, it doesn't help me when I have to use the telephone.

"So now you're telling me that you tested it yourself?"

I shook my head. "N-n-not exactly. B-b-but—"

"Maybe you think you can do my job better than me?"

Again I shook my head. I wanted to explain that things that should be simple to say sometimes weren't. This was why most people thought of me as a loner. It was too hard to talk to others. I had just found it easier to stay within my own thoughts than to make friends. Except for Gram.

"N-n-no," I said. "I d-d-don't. B-b-b-but—"

"Look," he said. "Wait here."

He walked heavily down the hallway. I heard a door open. Seconds later, he came back carrying a small box with the jars of water samples I had brought him. He plunked the box on the desk in front of me, scattering a small pile of paper.

"Hey!" the skinny woman in the red dress said. "Watch it. What if I had important letters and stuff in that pile that I needed to keep straight?"

"Fat chance, Doreen," he told her. "You type so slow you don't do more than a letter a day. Tough to get anything mixed up at that pace."

She put her hands on her hips and stared huffily at

him. "What's got into you, Fred? You never talk like that."

"Shut up," he told her. He grabbed a jar and opened it. He lifted it to his lips and swallowed a couple of mouthfuls of water. I watched his Adam's apple bob.

"See?" he said to me. "Nothing's wrong with it. Any more questions?"

I shook my head no. The questions I had I wouldn't ask him.

But I could tell something was wrong. This man was too defensive. He was rude, talking in a way he usually didn't. And he was working much too hard to prove to me the water was safe.

I decided right then and there that I would find another way to get the water samples tested.

And if it turned out something was wrong with the water from Gram's creek, I wanted to know why this guy was lying to me.

Seven

Coach Donaldson kept us pretty busy the next couple of days, so I didn't have a chance to do much about Gram's water samples. On Wednesday, Coach even called for a special practice, a half-hour earlier than usual. I didn't find out why until I had on my football gear and practice jersey and had joined a couple of guys on the sidelines of the field.

"Who's the new kid?" I heard Michael Shane ask as he gestured toward the coaches. Shane's a linebacker, built like a bull on steroids. And about as smart.

I looked in the direction he'd pointed. Old Coach Donaldson and Coach Pitt were talking to a tall kid with dark hair, dressed for practice. As they talked, the kid took short underhand tosses from Coach Pitt and rifled the ball twenty yards downfield to Jones and Powell, a couple of wide receivers in their junior year.

Coach Donaldson beamed as he watched the kid throw, proud as a father goo-gooing and ga-gaaing over a new baby. Coach Pitt was so happy, he didn't even yell at Powell for dropping two passes in a row.

"The new kid? Are you kidding?" Jamie McGuire, another linebacker, answered Shane. "Can't you tell by the guy's arm? That's Waymen Whitley. You know, all-state quarterback from Lexington."

Shane whistled. "Get out of here. Whalin' Waymen Whitley? What's *he* doing here?"

As always, I stayed at the edge of the conversation. Unless I was asked a direct question, it was easier on everyone if I just watched and listened.

"I heard his family just moved to Johnstown. Coach Donaldson must be thinking he just won the lottery."

That was an understatement. I'd read the newspapers too. They called this kid Whalin' because of all the lickings he'd laid on opposing teams. Waymen had taken Lexington High to the state finals in his freshman year. Whatever he had learned in losing the championship game that year had sunk in and stayed, because in his sophomore and junior years, he had taken the team right back to the finals and won both times. All three years he had been voted the league's Most Valuable Player. *Sports Illustrated* magazine had even featured him in a four-page article, predicting he could turn pro after only two years of college.

Michael Shane nudged me with his big elbow. "Good news for you, hey Linden? Finally a quarterback who can get you into the end zone."

I nodded. But I had worries. We were just a bunch of small-town players. What would a star like Whalin'

Waymen Whitley think about us—especially about a receiver like me who could barely talk?

Coach Donaldson noticed me on the sidelines. He waved me over.

I guess I was about to find out.

I had my helmet under my left arm as I trotted out to the center of the field.

When I reached Coach Donaldson and the others, Waymen glanced over at me. He didn't have the Hollywood kind of handsome face; his nose and chin were a little too big. But there was something in his eyes—a hunter's stare—that made him seem larger than life. Or maybe my imagination was just playing games with me because of all I had read about him.

"Waymen," Coach Donaldson said, "meet Roy Linden. Roy, meet Waymen Whitley, our new quarterback."

Waymen grinned. The hunter's stare disappeared as his eyes gave me a friendly twinkle. He stuck out a hand. I shook it. It felt big and rough with strong fingers. I found out later that he spent his summers working with bricklayers because his family didn't have much money.

"Roy Linden," Waymen said. "Good to meet you."

I nodded. He'd find out soon enough that I stuttered; I've never been in a hurry to make people wait for my slow replies, even with simple sentences.

"Coach Donaldson says you've got great speed and

good hands," Waymen said. "I'm looking forward to working with you."

I smiled and nodded again, still silent. I hated my stutter. Here was one of the greatest quarterbacks in high school football, and I looked like a dummy.

A few seconds later, Waymen just shrugged.

Coach Donaldson coughed to break the awkward moment. "Linden," Coach said, "run an out-pattern against Jones and Powell. I want to see if Whalin'—I mean, Waymen—can get you the ball against double coverage."

"Sure, Coach," Waymen said. "You want us to line up?"

"Yeah. That'd be good."

As I put on my helmet, Waymen squeezed my shoulder. "Knock 'em dead, sport. If you're half as good as I hear, we've got no problems."

In my mind, I answered, *Thanks. I know we'll knock 'em dead.* But my mouth said nothing.

Waymen frowned slightly as we walked to the thirty-yard line. Like he couldn't figure out why I was acting so rude.

The four of us stood all alone on the field—me and Waymen against Powell and Jones—with the coaches and the rest of the team watching.

"What kind of pattern you want to run?" Waymen asked. He said it loud enough that Steve Powell overheard.

"Shoot, Whalin'," Powell said, grinning like he was eating stolen watermelon. "Last thing you want to do is ask Linden a question. We'll be here all night w-w-w-aiting for th-th-the answer."

Part of me didn't blame Powell. He was probably nervous around this star quarterback and wanted to make an impression by picking on me.

"What do you mean?" Waymen asked, not sure about the joke.

"I s-s-s-t-tut-t-ter," I said. I tried to stand up straight and tall, like it was just a fact and I wasn't ashamed of it. If Waymen was going to laugh at me, I wasn't going to run from him like it hurt my feelings. I had done my best for years not to let people see my feelings get hurt.

"Not only does he stutter," Powell said, "but he's a loner too. Doesn't make friends with anyone."

Of course not. Friends meant having to talk. It was easier to stay in my own world, even if it was a little lonely.

Waymen said nothing to me. But the hunter's stare was back in his eyes when he spoke again.

"Here's the deal," he told Powell and Jones. "Linden's going to score a touchdown against you two. This play. This throw. He doesn't, and we owe you each a milk shake. He does, and you guys owe us."

Powell grinned, not noticing how cold and deadly Waymen's voice had gotten. "Deal."

Powell high-fived Jones, and they lined up opposite us.

Waymen stood close to me and spoke in a low voice. "Run an out-pattern, cut back. All you need is a half-step on them. At the hash mark, right side of the field on the other thirty-yard line, the ball will come in over your left shoulder. This'll be as easy as rolling out of bed."

A fifty-yard pass? As easy as rolling out of bed?

He banged the back of my helmet with his hand. "Ready?"

I gave him a thumbs-up.

It happened exactly as he had called it. He barked out a short signal, picked up the ball, and shuffled his feet as he waited for me to break loose. Powell and Jones back-pedaled a few yards. I ran out, cut back in at three-quarter speed and, just as they relaxed, put on the rocket burners and beelined at an angle toward the hash mark at the other thirty-yard line.

As my front foot crossed the line, Waymen's perfect spiral carried over my left shoulder and settled into my open hands. I let my speed carry me into the end zone, untouched.

I trotted back toward the center of the field. Powell and Jones stood hunched over, breathing hard.

I reached them about the same time as Waymen did.

"I'm a vanilla man when it comes to milk shakes," Waymen announced. "And I'm guessing you are, too—right, Linden?"

I nodded.

Waymen looked at Powell. "I got two things to say," Waymen said. "You can bring me and Linden our shakes at lunch tomorrow where everyone can see the payoff. That's the first thing."

"And the other?" Powell asked.

"Don't bother Linden here about the way he talks again."

The hunter's stare filled Waymen's eyes. Enough so that Powell shrank back.

"Believe me," Waymen told him. "You don't want to find out how angry I get when someone bothers a friend of mine."

 *Eight*

With permission from Mr. Engle, the biology and chemistry teacher, I was in the science lab at seven-thirty the next morning. He got me set up with the chemicals I needed, then went to the next room to grade some papers. If I needed him for anything, he was close by. But I was glad to have the lab to myself.

The lab was so quiet I could hear the ticking of the large clock above the door. Classes wouldn't start for a while yet, and the hallways were deserted except for the janitor and a couple of teachers.

I was still in the good mood that had stayed with me long after practice had ended. In fact, I had fallen asleep last night thinking about how it suddenly looked like the football season wouldn't be a disaster. I woke up this morning looking forward to lunch and the milk shakes that Waymen and I had earned from Powell and Jones.

What a dream, I thought, *Whalin' Waymen Whitley*

throwing me touchdown passes all season. University scholarship, here I come.

I also felt good about the fact that Waymen didn't seem bothered by my stuttering.

I was in such a good mood, I almost forgot how mad I was at the county health inspector for trying to make me believe nothing was wrong with the water from Gram's property.

Which, of course, was why I had gotten up so early to spend time in the science lab.

I was armed with a college chemistry textbook and another set of jars of water from Gram's creek and pond. I was ready to do some experiments. I didn't know exactly what I was looking for, but I couldn't just let this whole thing drop.

In front of me, in a stand on the table, were test tubes holding different acids. Not the kind of acids bad guys use in horror movies. But acids that mix with different chemicals and cause certain kinds of reactions.

I planned to mix the acids with small samples of the water. If I was lucky, crystals would form. Then maybe I could figure out what was in the water. Even if I couldn't get it exact, at least I'd have proof that there was something in the water.

I set twenty test tubes up in a rack and half filled each with Gram's water. Then I poured a different acid solution into each one. Nothing happened. But I wasn't disappointed. Not yet. Sometimes it takes a while for chemical reactions.

41

While I waited, I wandered over to the shelves against the far wall. They were filled with jars of stuff for the biology classes. The biggest jars held preserved pigs' hearts and cows' eyeballs—the stuff girls hate to dissect and guys love to joke around with to prove they aren't grossed out, even when they are. There was a complete snake skeleton. And a monkey skull.

Because I was in such a good mood, I picked up the monkey skull and held it in front of me—like I was the guy in *Hamlet*.

"To be or not to be," I said, starting the famous speech in my deepest, richest voice. "That is the question. Whether 'tis nobler in the mind to suffer the slings and arrows of outrageous misfortune. Or to take arms against a sea of troubles and by opposing, end them."

Not that I believe Shakespeare is everything those literature people say he is. I think those kind of people love going on and on about Shakespeare because the rest of us don't know much, and it makes those literature people feel smarter. But there are still some cool things worth learning.

Like this part in *Hamlet*: The guy is wondering if life is worth living, if he should fight his troubles.

"To die, to sleep, no more," I quoted, "and by sleep to say we end the heartache."

At this point in the play, Hamlet was really messed up. There had been murder in his family, and he thought he liked this girl but was afraid to like her too much.

"To die, to sleep," I repeated. "To sleep, perchance to dream. Aye, there's the rub. For in that sleep of death what dreams may come when we have shuffled off this mortal coil."

I was really getting into it, enjoying how I could speak without stuttering.

You see, I've learned some stuff about people who stutter. The guy who played Darth Vader, James Earl Jones, stuttered horribly when he was a kid. But something about saying someone else's words helped him not stutter.

Other people stutter when they speak, but not when they sing. And more often than not, people who stutter can talk perfectly fine when they're talking to a chair or a table or anything but another person.

It's enough to drive a person nuts. Sure, it takes a hundred muscles to speak. But why can everyone else do it so easily and not me? Except when I was alone.

"To grunt and sweat under a weary life," I said, gazing at the monkey skull just like Hamlet gazed at a human skull in the play. "But that the dread of something after death, the undiscovered country, from where no traveler returns. It puzzles the will."

I heard applause from behind me.

I turned, and there she was. A girl I had never seen before.

Nine

I put the monkey skull down so quickly that it toppled sideways and began to roll off the counter. I nearly tripped as I dived to catch it. Somehow I managed to miss banging my chin against the counter, and somehow the skull dropped safely into my hands.

More applause.

"Wow," the girl said. "Not only an actor, but an athlete too."

She was tall, close to my height. She wore jeans and a gray sweatshirt. Unlike a lot of girls at school, she hadn't hidden her face behind pounds of makeup. Her long hair was straight and brown. Some people might have thought her nose was a little too strong and her chin not so delicate. But with all of her features put together, and with the deep brown of her eyes, she was beautiful. Not cute. Beautiful.

I can hardly talk to people I know at the best of times. It's tougher to talk to strangers. But talk to a beautiful stranger I had never seen before? My tongue and mouth and throat froze.

I fumbled around as I set the monkey skull on the shelf where it belonged. I made sure it did not wobble or tip. Finally, I turned back to her.

Feeling like an idiot, I gave her a weak grin.

"I didn't mean to just barge in," she said. "But I was walking down the hallway. It's so quiet out there that I could hear you rehearsing. I like that part of *Hamlet,* too, so I couldn't help myself. I had to stop and listen. Is that okay?"

Sure, I said in my mind. I kept my stupid grin in place and nodded.

"Not to get serious or anything," she said, "but I think Shakespeare had it wrong. 'To be or not to be' is not the question. See, once you are, you are. Then the point is to find out *why* you are, and go from there."

She smiled. "What do you think?"

I think I can't possibly speak, I thought. But didn't say anything.

"I mean, there's that one part you just recited," she continued. "You know, about the undiscovered country. Can you repeat it for me?"

If I had stopped to think about it, I probably wouldn't have been able to. It's like walking down a set of stairs. You never stop to think about it. You just do it. If you did think about it, you'd probably be afraid to. After all, to go down a set of stairs, you have to put one foot into empty space and launch your body after it. You have to trust that the foot is going to come down in a safe spot and keep you from falling.

"To grunt and sweat under a weary life." I stopped in total surprise. I wasn't alone, but I had spoken perfectly. No stutters. "But that the dread of something after death, the undiscovered country, from where no traveler returns. It puzzles the will."

"Yes," she said, nodding. "That part. It's beautiful poetry, but if you believe the body has a soul, it's perfect nonsense, because the undiscovered country— heaven—is waiting for us to explore. Hamlet would have had a lot more hope. Right?"

I didn't trust my voice. I was still totally amazed that I had managed to recite a difficult piece of Shakespeare in front of her without stuttering.

She didn't need an answer; she kept on speaking. "Anyway," she said, "you might be curious why I like Shakespeare. It's simple. I'm into drama. I want to be a Broadway actress."

Sure, I said, again in my mind. *I can see that.*

"I'm guessing you must be in the high school drama club. As good as you are, I mean. I'll probably see you there. I plan to join right after school. I know it's a little late to join, but my family and I just moved to Johnstown."

Her voice was bubbly. "You see, my dad just got a new job with the Johns Corporation. It was a great offer, a total surprise, almost like winning the lottery. I'm so glad we're here."

I nodded more. Feeling, as usual, like an idiot.

"I'm looking forward to making a lot of new friends. I'd like to get to know you better." She smiled and moved closer to me, extending her hand. "Okay?"

I shook her hand. I hadn't had to say anything. But I felt dazed. *Was this how a moose that steps in front of a moving train feels?*

With another smile, she turned and walked away.

At the doorway, she stopped. "I almost forgot," she said. "My name is Elizabeth. Elizabeth Whitley. I'm in tenth grade."

Whitley? Whalin' Waymen Whitley's sister?

She waited for me to tell her my name.

I would have tried. I hated trying to tell people my name. When I can't get it out quickly, I look dumb. Like I don't even know my name. But for her, I would have tried.

If I hadn't noticed the water samples on the lab table. Crystals had formed in one of the test tubes!

I pointed, trying to tell her with body language that something important had happened.

She didn't understand. Her smile dimmed.

I was too excited to get a single word out.

Her smile became a puzzled frown, and she walked back into the hallway.

Leaving me much more alone than I had been before.

Finding out that there really was something in the water suddenly seemed like a second place prize.

Ten

Friday night again. Second game of the season. Another pep talk. This time from Coach Donaldson.

"Boys," he said. "I'm not going to say much tonight. I think you're excited enough as it is, having a new quarterback."

Donaldson gave Schenley a big smile. "Schenley, I expect you're the most excited of all. For a year now, you've been asking me to find someone else to quarterback so's you could play runningback. But you did what we asked because you were the best we had. I am happy to say, tonight you get to shift positions."

"Thanks, Coach," Schenley said.

Coach Donaldson lowered his eyes and spoke to the floor. "Boys, this second part—I didn't know if I should tell you."

He lifted his head again. "But I don't want any of you making the same mistake, so the earlier I tell you, the better. Please listen up."

The seriousness in his voice got our full attention.

"You'll notice I don't have a wad of chewing tobacco in my mouth," he said. "That's because I gave it up. Doctor told me this morning I've got a cancer on my tongue."

If possible, the room got even quieter.

"They're going to have to operate. I'll lose a piece of my tongue with the tumor, and I probably won't be able to speak too good. So this might be my last season as a coach."

He looked at us without flinching. "Don't feel sorry for me, though. It could be way worse. Doc says I'll be fine after the operation. Some folks, he told me, lose their lips or teeth or cheeks, even a piece of their jawbones. Some die because the cancer eats its way down their throats."

He coughed. "Anyway, I got two last things to say tonight. First one is, it ain't cool to chew."

He gave us a grin. "And second, knock off those sad looks and get out there and play hard. If this is my last season, let's make it a winning one!"

We ran out to the field with two big differences from last week's game. We were playing out of town. And we were armed with one of the best quarterbacks in the state.

The Coluth Coal Miners finished third in the division last year, and some newspapers had predicted they would be even better this year. What they really had going for them was a monstrous defensive line-backer named Robert Smith. It was a boring name, but most people called him Chain Saw. And he lived up to his nickname.

First of all, he could rip through an offensive line exactly like a chain saw. He easily weighed 250 pounds, had the sweetness of a grizzly with his leg in a trap, and did his best to hurt opposing players whenever he thought he could get away with it.

There was another reason people called him Chain Saw. He'd spent six months on probation for losing his temper and using one to destroy a car. Some guy had insulted him at school. That night, Chain Saw had pushed the guy's car five miles to an empty field and cut it in half with a chain saw.

"That's the guy, huh?" Waymen asked me as we moved onto the field.

Chain Saw was number 66, in the green and white uniform of the Coal Miners.

"H-hard to m-m-miss," I said.

"Yeah," Waymen agreed.

As we stared at Chain Saw, he shuffled up the field toward us, carrying his helmet in his hand. All our guys gave him plenty of room. He stopped in front of me and Waymen.

"So you're the hotshot," Chain Saw said to Waymen. His voice was surprisingly high. But I'll bet no one bugged him about it. Not with that face that looked like it had stopped sledgehammers.

"Waymen Whitley," Waymen said, sticking out his

hand. "And this is my friend Roy Linden. Have a good game."

Chain Saw worked up a good gob and spit on Waymen's left shoe.

"I'm going to be all over you like a nightmare," Chain Saw said.

Waymen smiled sweetly. "I must admit, you look the part already."

Chain Saw frowned, not quite sure if he'd been insulted.

Behind him, the ref blew the whistle.

Chain Saw snarled at us and headed back to his team.

We received the kickoff. I returned it to our forty-yard line before getting buried by a wave of green and white. Before I could stand, Chain Saw kicked me in the ribs.

"Don't get fancy," Chain Saw said. "I'll chew you up."

I got to my knees, hardly able to breathe it hurt so much. I looked around to see if the referee had noticed the kick. The referee, however, was facing the other way. Then I realized: hometown field, hometown referee. The ref had made sure he was looking away.

It turned out not to matter.

Waymen was so good, he drove us down the field in five plays—three of them passes to me.

By the end of the third quarter, we had scored four touchdowns, three point afters, and a field goal, to give us a 30–21 lead. Altogether, I had twelve receptions and three touchdowns. Waymen was proving exactly how good he was. He threw like he was pointing a rifle, carrying the ball he could run like a scalded fox, and when their linebackers broke through, he dodged them as if they were stalled trucks.

All of it was good.

The bad part was Chain Saw.

By the end of the third quarter, Chain Saw had kicked me twice more, spit on two other players, poked his fingers in the eyes of another three. He was getting angrier and angrier because he hadn't once been able to tackle Waymen.

In the huddle at first and ten on their thirty-yard line, toward the end of the quarter, Waymen looked around at us.

"You boys tired of that ugly slab of meat wearing number 66?"

We didn't have to answer.

"Good," he said. "Let's go for a field goal on the fourth down. First three downs, let Chain Saw through the line."

"Like we've been stopping him," one of our offensive guards said.

Waymen grinned and clapped his hands to break the huddle.

When our center snapped the ball, Waymen backpedaled, waiting for Chain Saw. He lumbered through, arms windmilling from his massive body.

Waymen played him like a matador playing a bull.

Waymen sidestepped, but left one leg in place so it looked like an accident when Chain Saw tripped. Chain Saw fell so hard that his faceguard plowed the field.

Waymen fired a short pass to me. I was hit hard for a gain of only a yard.

Next huddle, Waymen reminded the guards to let Chain Saw through again.

This time, Chain Saw was bellowing with rage as he tried to tackle Waymen. Waymen dodged once and spun around, going backward. Then as Chain Saw tried to cover more ground, Waymen fired the ball hard at Chain Saw's helmet—so hard that the point of the football squeezed through and popped Chain Saw on the nose.

That left us at third and eight, with Chain Saw so mad that we could almost hear the grinding of his teeth above the roar of the crowd.

"Let him through again," Waymen told us in the huddle, "I think I've got him where I want him."

And, once more, the guards let him through.

This time, as Waymen back-pedaled, he slipped. Or, as he told me later, pretended to slip. He fell square on his back.

Chain Saw came roaring to dive on Waymen with all 250 pounds of anger.

As I watched, green and white covered Waymen, the green and white of a guy who had broken the legs of three different players in the last two seasons.

But seconds later, Chain Saw rolled away, groaning

in agony. He couldn't get to his feet. It took four men and a stretcher to get him off the field.

I trotted over to Waymen.

"Wh-what h-happened?" I asked.

"Tough break," he said. "I sort of lifted my knee to protect myself as he came down. And he sort of landed on it. And it sort of hit him somewhere below the belly button."

He shook his head. "I sort of feel bad about it."

"Th-that h-he's out of the game?"

"Nope," Waymen said, grinning. "I sort of feel bad about my poor knee. He does weigh a lot, you know."

I grinned back.

We made the field goal and never looked back, winning the second game of the season 40–21.

Things were looking good.

At least on the football field.

Eleven

I decided that Monday after football practice would be a good time to stop by the newspaper office. I drove my truck from the high school and parked downtown.

The *Johnstown Journal* was in a small building just off Main Street, squeezed between a men's clothing store and a small restaurant. The late afternoon sun bounced off the front window, and as I walked to the door, I saw my reflection.

It did not make me feel better. What I saw was a high school kid armed with a jar of water and a notebook. I wondered again whether this would actually work. But I didn't know what else to do, especially since the county health inspector clearly wasn't going to help me.

I took a deep breath and pushed the front door open.

A bell tinkled.

The office looked like something you would see in an old black-and-white movie. The one big desk in the corner belonged to the *Journal*'s only reporter, a big-bellied man named Eldon Mawther. He had a type-writer on his desk. An old rotary telephone—the kind that had a circle you spun to dial the num-bers—sat beside it. Framed black-and-white photos hung on the walls behind him, showing him as a much younger man shaking hands with different people, including one with President Nixon during his visit to Johnstown.

Eldon Mawther stood up when I walked in. Unlike his younger self in the photos, he was now nearly bald. He grew the hair on the side of his head long, greased it, and combed it over the top. He always wore dark pants with suspenders and a white shirt and a bow tie. He had worked for the newspaper for nearly forty years. I knew all that because he came to every Cobra football game, and he spent more time telling us things than he did asking us questions.

"Roy Linden," he said in a booming voice with fake friendliness. "How's our star receiver?"

I smiled for an answer. This was one of the few times it was good that I couldn't speak my thoughts. Two weeks ago, he wouldn't have been this friendly. Two weeks ago, I was just another high school foot-ball player to him. But that was before Whalin' Waymen Whitley showed up and threw me three touchdown passes in one game. If Eldon Mawther wanted to be my friend just because he suddenly thought I was a star, he wasn't a friend much worth having.

And there was another reason I just smiled. I had something important to say, and I didn't want to mess up how I said it.

I'd been thinking a lot about my stuttering since Waymen's sister had caught me quoting Shakespeare. Especially about how I had surprised myself by quoting more of it with her right in front of me.

It was just more of the mystery that faced people who stutter. A famous country music singer named Mel Tillis can sing perfectly, but when he speaks, he stutters.

For me, I wondered if there was something about speaking from a memorized script that got me past my stutter. And I was about to find out.

"Good afternoon, Mr. Mawther," I said. "I've got some interesting news for you."

Hah! It worked!

I had written out my own script and pretended it was a scene in a play where a kid talks to a newspaper reporter. I had memorized the words and acted them in front of a mirror, just like I had done with the Shakespeare stuff. And now, I was actually following my script without stuttering!

"Let me tell you, son," he said, chuckling. "You don't need to bring me the news. You and Whalin' Waymen just keep playing like you did this weekend. That kind of news will take care of itself. And I'll keep on writing it the way I see it."

He scratched his belly. "You like that story I wrote about Waymen Whitley?"

"Sir," I said, still playing my part. I held up the jar. "There's something wrong with this water."

He frowned. "What's water got to do with my story? I'm thinking it was good enough to sell to *Sports Illustrated*. Jed down at the barbershop says the same thing. Did Waymen Whitley happen to mention whether he read it himself? I didn't get a chance to ask him after the football game Friday."

"Fact is, sir," I continued, setting my jar of water on his desk, "I believe the story goes beyond that."

"Me too," Eldon Mawther said, no longer scratching his belly, but rubbing it like it was a cat. "I've always said I could do some good writing if there was anything worth writing about in this town. And Whalin' Whitley fits the bill, all right. So tell me what you thought of my story."

"Down at the county offices, an inspector told me there was nothing wrong with the water, but—"

"Water?" Eldon Mawther wrinkled up his round face, looking like he might sneeze. "Water? We're talking football, boy. What's water got to do with anything?"

Actually, *he* was talking football. I was sticking to my memorized script. I was afraid I'd start stuttering if I answered his questions.

I held up my notebook. "And sir," I said, "here are my notes on my own testing of the water."

"Boy, did a tackle knock a nut loose in your head?"

I had my script, and I was sticking to it. "The water

sample was taken from a spring on the property of Claire Linden. While I could not discover exactly what chemical is in it, it has killed birds and fish. Somewhere, something is leaking into that water."

Eldon Mawther had stopped rubbing his big belly. I noticed rings under his armpits where old sweat had dried.

"There is a story here," I finished. "A story about the chemicals. And a story about why the county health inspector tried to make me believe there is nothing wrong with the water."

I set the notebook beside the jar filled with water on his desk. "The story is yours, sir. Take the water and the notebook. It's all you need to get started."

I let out a deep breath. It had taken a lot of concentration to follow my script.

The reporter eased himself onto the corner of his desk. He stretched out his suspenders with his thumbs. He stared at me for nearly half a minute.

Finally, he spoke. His voice was flat. Not friendly at all. "There ain't no story, boy."

Of all the things I had prepared for, this answer was not one of them. No story? I had seen crystals of something form in the water. And while I had seen the county health inspector drink it, I wondered if he had switched the samples first. I had written all of my test results in the notebook. What did this man mean, there was no story?

"Listen to me good," he said. "There ain't no story. And if there was a story, there still ain't no story."

"B-but how can you say th-th-that?" No script to follow. My stutter was back. "Th-th-ere is s-something wrong with th-th-th-the water. I kn know it."

"Didn't I just say listen to me good? Let it drop."

Let it drop?

I repeated my thoughts out loud. "L-l-let it dr-drop?" He stood and pushed me to the door.

"Stick to football, boy," he said. "You've got a future there. Now if you don't mind, I have deadlines."

"B-b-but—"

"Good-bye," he said. "Don't visit again unless you want to talk football."

Twelve

I walked back to my truck, my head down and my face burning red with anger.

What did he mean, there was no story?

I had seen the dead birds. I knew there was something in the water. My tests in the chem lab had proved that. I only wish I knew enough to be able to pinpoint *what* was in the water. The high school chem lab didn't have everything I needed to do that.

The county health inspector had told me there was nothing wrong with the water. But I knew he'd either done a bad job of testing it, or he had lied to me.

And now the *Journal*'s reporter was doing his best to ignore what I had to say too.

Something strange was happening. This *was* a story.

The trouble for me was I didn't know where else to go. If the county health inspector wasn't interested, and the *Johnstown Journal* wasn't interested, who could I get to help me find out what was going on?

By the time I got back to my truck, I was mad enough to know the answer.

Who could find out what was going on?

I could.

The next day, I had a study period just before lunch. That meant I could leave school early if I needed to. Which I did.

Again, the sky was a perfect blue; the leaves had just started to turn colors. A small breeze pushed at my hair as I walked across the parking lot to my truck.

It was a good day to go for a drive in the hills and visit Gram, a good day to spend some peaceful time at her cabin.

Unfortunately, I couldn't. Because if I didn't do something about her poisoned water, her small part of the world would no longer be as beautiful.

Halfway across the parking lot, I heard someone call my name.

I stopped and turned to see Waymen Whitley running toward me, tall and lean and graceful like the star quarterback that he was. Because most kids were still in class, he was the only other person in the parking lot.

I waited for him.

"Hey," he said, when he caught up with me, "where you going?"

If anyone else had asked me, I might have shrugged

to try to get out of answering. But Waymen seemed to really care about people. Including me.

"J-j-johns C-c-corporation."

"No kidding," he said. "That's where my dad works. Yours too?"

I shook my head. "My p-p-parents d-died when I was th-three."

"Sorry to hear it, man. That must have been pretty awful."

"Y-yeah." But he wouldn't want to hear how I cried myself to sleep all those nights when I was little.

For a moment, it was awkward, with neither of us knowing what to say.

"So," he finally said, "you want company? I don't have another class until two."

Usually, I keep to myself. I prefer the quiet conversations in my head over the stumbling conversations I have with other people. But there was no way to say no without looking like a jerk. And I remembered how much I'd liked it when he called me a friend in front of Powell and Jones at his first practice.

"S-sounds g-g-good," I said.

And I hoped it would be.

Thirteen

We were at the stop sign at the end of the parking lot when Waymen spoke next.

"No one in school or on the team knows it," Waymen said. "But for a long time I could hardly read. It's still kind of hard. And it drives me nuts."

I looked over at him, not sure why he was telling me this or what I should say back to him. He was resting easy, his big hands on his knees.

"When I was a kid," he continued, "I hated it when teachers would ask me to read something out loud to the class. It would take me forever to get through a sentence. Even then, I'd get half the words wrong. Still sometimes drives me nuts, trying to get through some of my homework assignments. 'Specially now in high school."

Our windows were down, and the wind felt good against my face. I listened to him carefully.

"Anyway," Waymen said, "people made me feel

stupid because I couldn't read. Then we figured out that I have dyslexia. Something in my brain makes me see letters and words backward. I had to learn other ways of looking at letters and letter patterns to see words. Still can't spell very well."

"I'd h-hate that," I said. "R-reading is one of the b-best th-things that's happened to me. I c-can get lost in a g-good book and not c-come out for hours."

"Because it's easier to read than talk?" he asked me.

I slowed down for a traffic light. I waited until the truck had stopped to look over at him.

He smiled before I could get mad. "Hey," he said, "for me it's easier to talk than read. And if you and I have to both pretend you don't stutter, it's going to be tough to be friends."

"Wh-wh-wh-why do you th-th-think w-w-we're going to be f-friends?" I didn't ask it in a mean way. But in a curious way. And he understood.

He grinned. "One, you're the best receiver I've ever seen. No one in the state can catch and run like you. I'd be a dumb quarterback not to make friends with the guy who's going to help us both set a single-season record for touchdowns."

He didn't say it like it was cocky. More like he really believed we would set a record. And that I should believe it too.

His grin turned more serious. "And two, I'm like you. Words mess me up. And people have hassled me about it. Why do you think I got so mad at Powell at my first practice? For what it's worth, I'd seriously think about trading. You take my dyslexia and I'll take your stutter. I mean, it's a lot easier to get a university degree with a stutter than it is with a reading problem."

"Wh-why would you n-need a degree?" I joked. It was becoming easier to talk to him now that I knew he didn't care about my stuttering. "You can m-make m-millions as a pro quarterback."

He pointed. I looked up. The red light had turned back to green. I hit the gas and the truck moved through the intersection.

"What if I get hurt?" he said. "Then what? All my life, I've watched my mom and dad struggle because they couldn't make much money. I promised them I would get an education, and I aim to deliver."

I remembered what Elizabeth, his sister, had told me about her dad getting a new job.

"Your s-sister s-said the Johns C-corporation offering your dad this job was like w-winning a lottery."

"Are you kidding?" he said. "It's unbelievable. Dad is making triple what he was before."

Waymen frowned. "When did you talk to my sister?"

"In th-the science lab one m-morning."

He slapped his leg. "That was you? The guy quoting Shakespeare? She told us all about it."

"L-long story," I said. We were getting close to the Johns Corporation.

"But you . . ."

"S-stutter?"

"Yeah," he answered.

I took a deep breath. "To be or not to be. That is the question. Whether 'tis nobler in the mind to suffer the slings and arrows of outrageous misfortune. Or to take arms against a sea of troubles and by opposing, end them."

"I don't get it," he said. "How do you do that?"

"I'm n-not sure," I said. I explained how stuttering is a mystery to doctors and to people who stutter. "Acting, r-reciting lines, is d-different for m-me from sp-speaking, I guess."

He grinned. It was an easy grin to like. "Then do more acting," he said. "I wish my dyslexia was as easy to beat."

I flicked my turn signal for the right into the Johns Corporation parking lot. "M-more acting," I said. "R-right."

As if it would ever happen. Me, speaking in front of an audience full of strangers?

I pulled the truck into a parking spot near the shiny glass and brick of the main building.

"I never did ask," he said. "What exactly are you doing here?"

"Another l-long story," I answered. "N-not a b-big deal."

It was, of course. But it wasn't something I figured would be a big deal to him.

Later, I would find out how wrong I was.

Fourteen

The main offices of the Johns Corporation were in a two-story building about a block long. A wide sidewalk led to a wide set of steps. At the top of the steps, just before the glass doors, a decorative fountain burbled. Altogether, it was an impressive building for a town as small as Johnstown.

"Wh-hat does your d-dad d-do here?" I asked Waymen as we walked past the splashing fountain.

"Back in Lexington," Waymen said, "he worked as a mechanic for a small service station. Here, he supervises all of the mechanics who work on the company vehicles."

I whistled. That would be some job. Between the company cars and the trucks they used in the coal fields, there was a lot to take care of. He probably had a lot of people working for him.

"His office is somewhere in there," Waymen said. "Maybe later, we can visit."

"If y-you w-want, go ahead," I said. I didn't want Waymen watching as I tried to talk to strangers. "We can m-meet back here in h-half an hour."

Waymen looked at me with a smile. "I think I'd rather stay with you. I'm curious to see what you're doing here."

The security guard at the front desk was curious too. Behind him, the building split into two hallways. It was quiet with the hushed kind of whispers an expensive air conditioner makes.

"What is your business here?" the guard asked. He was tall and broad shouldered and very serious in his uniform. "Do you have an appointment with someone?"

Waymen looked at me. I did my best to answer.

"I w-want to t-talk to someone about m-m-maps," I said.

"Maps?"

"C-coal m-m-ine m-maps," I said, hating how my stutter got worse at his stern look.

"The Johns Corporation is not a public company," the guard said. "The information on those maps is not for just anyone who walks in off the street."

"I j-j-just w-w-want t-to t-talk—"

"There is nothing to talk about," he snapped, impatient with my slowness.

"Sir," Waymen said, "I know this is not a usual request. It's more of a school project. We go to Johnstown High School. This is Roy Linden, and my name is Waymen Whitley. We—"

"Whalin' Waymen Whitley?" the guard said. He stared at Waymen. "I should have recognized you from the newspaper. Your old man works here, don't he?"

The guard snapped his fingers. "And Roy Linden. I know that name. You scored three touchdowns! I wish I could have seen the game last Friday. But being as it was out of town, I couldn't. What do you think about this upcoming game against the Cougars? From what I hear they're an even better team than they were last year. If you guys can beat them, this whole side of the state is going to have to sit up and take notice. I mean, you guys could have a shot at the league title."

Waymen grinned. "League? Let's talk state. Put Roy here in a pair of Nikes and he can run down a deer. A fella doesn't have to be much of a quarterback with someone like him as a target."

Waymen talked football with the guard for a few more minutes, long enough to make him happy. When the conversation got around to our "school" project again, the guard lifted his phone to call ahead for us.

"Sign in," the guard instructed us. He handed us a clipboard. There was a place for our names and the time of our arrival. There was another space to mark the time when we left.

"Down the hall to the first turn, then go right," the guard said. "Look for door 128."

"Thank you, sir," Waymen said.

We walked away.

"This *is* a school project," Waymen said. "Right?"

"N-now it is," I answered. I'd write this up as part of a report for science. It made me wonder why I hadn't thought of it before. "B-biology."

"Then count me in on it," Waymen said. "I can use some extra credit in biology."

"D-deal," I said.

About a minute later it looked like we didn't have much of a deal, after all. That's how long it took us to talk to the guy in office number 128. And to get thrown out.

Fifteen

Before the guy could grab my shirt and push me out the door, though, we'd had to get past his secretary to see him.

"Waymen Whitley, ma'am," Waymen said to the woman behind the desk who was facing a computer monitor. She was middle-aged, with a round face and a sweet smile. "And my friend, Roy Linden. I believe the security guard just called about our arrival."

"Yes he did." She gave us more of her sweet smile. "You can go on in. Mr. Webber is expecting you."

She pointed at the open door behind her. The room looked bright from the sunshine streaming through the window. I led the way.

Mr. Webber's desk, shiny and dark brown, filled half the office. Shelves covered with books lined one wall. A photo of him and a woman and two kids sat on top of one of the shelves.

Just like in the photo, he was a large man, wearing

a dark suit. His dark hair was neatly cut. He wore wide glasses on a big nose.

He stood up and smiled a greeting at both of us as he extended his hand.

"M-m-my name is Roy L-l-inden," I said. "I w-w-was h-hoping you c-could h-help m-me with c-coal m-mine m-m-maps."

His face darkened instantly into an angry frown. Faster than I could have believed possible for such a big man, he came around his desk.

That's when he grabbed my shirt and dragged me back through the doorway, past the secretary's desk on his way to the hallway. He was such a big man and I was so surprised, I didn't even try to fight.

Waymen followed, his mouth wide with shock.

"Mr. Webber!" the secretary said. "Mr. Webber! What is going on?"

Mr. Webber paused, his strong hands still squeezing my shirt tight against me.

"N-n-n-nobody w-w-w-walks into m-m-my office and m-m-m-makes fun of m-m-m-me!" he said to her. "I don't h-h-have to p-p-put up with it!"

"B-b-b-b-b . . ." I was too flustered to get much past the first word of what I was trying to say. "B-b-b-but y-you d-d-d-d—"

I just made him angrier.

"Th-th-that's enough!" he yelled. "G-g-g-get out you p-p-p-punk!"

"Sir! Sir!" Waymen shouted, moving in front of us and waving to get his attention. "Sir!"

Mr. Webber glared at him.

"He's not making fun of you, sir," Waymen said. "He—"

Waymen lost it. He started to giggle. His giggle became laughter.

"He—" Waymen could hardly speak, he was laughing so hard.

It gave me a chance to work a few words out.

"I s-s-s-tutter t-t-oo," I said. "R-r-r-really."

"R-r-r-really?" Mr. Webber asked.

"R-r-r-really," I said.

Hearing the two of us stutter back and forth just made Waymen laugh harder. I could tell he wasn't laughing at me or Mr. Webber, but at the situation. I never wanted people to feel sorry or embarrassed for me because of my stutter. I was glad Waymen could laugh about it. Because it was funny.

I started to laugh too.

Finally, Mr. Webber joined us. He laughed so hard that he had to lean against his secretary's desk.

Every time either one of us tried to speak again, our stutters made us all howl louder.

It got so bad that people from other offices stuck their heads in the door to see what was so funny. That, of course, just made us laugh even louder. Mr. Webber had to wave them away as he wiped tears of laughter from his eyes.

It took ten minutes for us to settle down. Mr. Webber apologized and said he had had a bad morning and he was sorry for getting so mad so quickly.

I told him I didn't mind because I understood how frustrating it could get.

As it turned out, I couldn't have asked for a better way to start off with the one man who could give me the most answers at the Johns Corporation. He felt so bad about how we'd met that he helped me way more than he should have. He gave me stuff the public never sees.

When Waymen and I left his office, we had maps of all the mine shafts—old and new—that the Johns Corporation had dug anywhere near Gram's cabin.

And those maps gave me the information I wanted.

Sixteen

The next day I knew I would have to wait until after practice to drive up into the hills to Gram's cabin. As usual, my day at school was full and went by very quickly. My mind didn't stay on what I might learn by listening to my teachers, however. It kept wandering to caves and underground rivers.

Kentucky is famous for its caves. About eighty-five miles west of Louisville is the Mammoth Cave, a tourist attraction. It's actually a bunch of connected caves—more than three hundred miles' worth at five different levels.

The caves were made when limestone—Kentucky is full of it—got dissolved by water. Underground rivers cut their way beneath many of the mountains in the area. The Mammoth Cave formed when a number of underground rivers and streams flowed through, including the Echo River, which comes to the surface and eventually flows into the Green River.

Around our town, according to the Johns Corporation maps, an underground river fed the creek near Gram's cabin. And, according to the maps, that same underground river passed near an inactive coal mining shaft. It looked like the shaft had been closed down for years.

If there was something toxic in that shaft, maybe it had leaked into the underground river and had been carried into Gram's pond. That might explain why small animals were dying on Gram's property.

All of the pieces were nearly together for me. Except, of course, for discovering what that shaft held and how it got there.

And I hoped I would not have to find out the hard way.

After practice ended, I showered and changed as quickly as I could. When Waymen asked if I wanted to head out with a couple of guys for a milk shake, I told him I needed to visit my grandmother.

He gave me his all-star grin and told me to watch out for the Big Bad Wolf.

I was still smiling about that as I left the high school.

I was still smiling as I practiced my Shakespeare quotes into my tape recorder as I usually did when I drove.

I stopped smiling a mile later when I noticed a black car behind me. It had stayed with me, even after

I had turned two or three times. The car was maybe a quarter mile back with smoked-glass windows.

Normally, I might not even have noticed. But after the weirdness with the county health inspector and the newspaper reporter, and with my mind on underground rivers and possible pollution from a big coal mining company, the black car made me nervous.

I shut my tape recorder off. I turned left at the next corner, turned left again a block later, and finally, made another left back onto the same street I had started on. The black car stayed with me the entire time.

It *was* following me.

I didn't know what to do.

Would the driver try something crazy once I was on the lonely road up in the hills?

I grabbed my tape recorder again. This time, however, I didn't practice Shakespeare when I spoke. Instead, I said, "F-f-five-th-thirty-f-five P.M." I was so nervous that my stutter made it hard to talk. "A c-c-ar is f-following. B-black. L-late model F-f-ord, probably a C-crown Vict-t-t-oria. I w-will k-keep rec-c-ord of events."

I felt stupid doing this, like I was in some sort of movie. But if something did happen—like the black car stopping me and the driver trying something—I would report as much as I could then hide the tape recorder under the seat. Whoever found it later would at least know what had happened.

As I drove, I had another idea.

The car kept following as I made two more turns.

Right to the parking lot of the sheriff's office. Two squad cars sat in front. I stopped beside them, and got out of the truck.

Hands on my hips, I waited for the black car to approach.

It slowed at the entrance to the parking lot but then kept going. I could not see inside the dark windows. I had no idea what the driver looked like. Or if there were any passengers.

At the next corner, the car's taillights blinked red and the black car turned.

I waited a few minutes. The car did not come back.

I got back in my truck and began driving again. I kept a close eye on my rearview mirror. I did not see the car again, and I made it safely to Gram's cabin.

There, I discovered the Johns Corporation had beat me to her.

Seventeen

Th-three quarters of a m-million dollars?" I asked. I wasn't sure if I could trust my ears with all the buzzing of the insects in the woods around us.

Gram and I sat in the rockers on her front porch, watching the last of the day's light. Fireflies glowed on and off around bushes in front of the cabin. It would have been a postcard-perfect moment of peace. Except for what Gram had just told me.

"Yes, sir," she said. "A feller in a black car drove up the lane this very morning and said he was from the Johns Corporation and—"

I put up my hands as if trying to hold back a stampede.

"B-black car?"

"Roy, you seem particular hard of hearing today. Was it that you got banged in the head playing football? Tell me you've been wearing a helmet in practice."

She laughed at her joke. I did not.

Black car. Johns Corporation. Where I had been yesterday. Where I had signed in and out with the security guard, leaving my name *for anyone to read.* It made sense. They knew I was looking into all this. And in another way, it didn't make any sense.

"Roy?" Gram was asking. "I said, tell me you've been wearing a helmet in practice."

I nodded. "Th-this fellow . . ."

"I tell you I smelled him for a polecat the minute he got out of that car . . . wearing those shiny leather shoes, stepping light as if he were scared to get mud on them. Some weasel-faced guy with a missing tooth. He had a lemon-sucking grin across his face and he flat out offered me a half million dollars for my cabin and land."

"B-but you just t-told me th-three quarters of a m-million."

"Sure, I did." Gram gave me a lemon-sucking grin of her own. "He started at a half million. I kept bumping him up to see how high he'd go. Just 'cause I'm old, don't mean my brains have leaked out of my head."

I grinned. "What d-did you t-tell him? I m-m-mean with that kind of m-money, you could b-buy a lot of b-bottled water."

She knew I was joking. "Sure I'll do that," she said, "as soon as the wildlife around here learns to drink from bottles too."

I nodded grimly. Gram was always telling me that God gave us the world to take care of. If she let the company buy her off, the wildlife would surely suffer.

Gram rocked for a few minutes, staring off at the low clouds. I knew better than to interrupt.

"Roy," she finally said, "I was tempted. Not for myself, mind you. I have all I need, and I don't hanker none to die rich. But you know how bad I want you to go to college. That much money? A person could do a powerful lot of good with it."

She rocked a bit more. "Still, I asked myself what Jesus would do. And I remember how he was tempted in the desert when the devil offered him the whole world. Jesus didn't tell himself that all he had to do was take the devil's money, even though it would be enough to provide all the hospitals and schools and food and clothes the poor people needed. No sir. Jesus looked that devil in the eye and told him to get lost. No amount of money would be worth losing your soul."

Gram turned her wrinkled smile toward me. "Believing ain't really believing if you don't practice it. I told that polecat I had no interest in dealing with the Johns Corporation. When I asked him if his offer had anything to do with my water going bad, he jumped like a snake had latched onto his hind end."

Gram never failed to impress me. To figure out that connection, I'd had to deal with the county health inspector and the newspaper reporter, test the water myself, and look at a detailed map showing how the water that fed her spring flowed past a nearby Johns Corporation mine shaft.

I told her how impressed I was.

She shook her head sadly. "A bag full of hammers

would have been smart enough to put the Johns Corporation and my bad water together. Why else would someone from there offer me ten times what the property is worth?"

I suddenly realized that my questions about the water had reached someone important in the corporation. Someone who could send a man in a black car to follow me. Someone who could send a man out to Gram's cabin with an offer of money.

I told Gram about Fred, the county health inspector, and how he discounted my tests on the water.

"Shoot, Roy," she said. "Everyone knows Fred at the county office has a weakness for betting on horses. That, plus he's third cousin once removed from the Johns family. Wouldn't be hard for them to get him to turn a blind eye. My guess is that he saw something in the water and went straight to the top of the company, and flat out asked for a payoff to keep his mouth shut."

I told Gram about Eldon Mawther.

She clucked her tongue. "Roy, you're a babe among wolves. The Johns Corporation owns the *Journal*. A good old boy like Eldon, he ain't interested in causing trouble with the people who butter his bread."

I took out the map and showed her what I had learned.

"Young man," she said after I showed her the underground river that fed her spring. "It's a miracle you got this map. The man who gave it to you must not have known why you wanted it. And he must have taken a shine to you."

I smiled. I'd tell her that story later.

"Look," she said, "I don't want you giving up on this. If a wrong has been done, it's got to be fixed. And if no one is going to help you fix it, you've got to do it yourself. This here is almost enough to call a state authority. Maybe even the FBI. They ain't afraid of the Johns Corporation."

"A-almost enough?" I asked.

"Almost," she said firmly. "What you really need to know is what's in that mine shaft and how it got there."

I was afraid of that.

"'Course," she said, "that ain't nothing I want you to do. Not in a place as dangerous as a mine shaft. I've got some kin around here that owe me favors. Folks that work in the coal mine and know their way around the shafts. I'll ask around real quiet and get them to find out."

She looked me straight in the eye. "Promise me now that you'll sit pretty and wait. I don't want you trying anything as foolish as doing it yourself."

"I promise," I said.

I meant that promise too. I wondered if I should tell her how that black car had followed me.

I decided not to.

No sense in two of us worrying.

Besides, I told myself, this was just about money. Not about hurting people.

Right?

Eighteen

Friday night. Game three of the season. Back home.

The stands were jammed with people. As we trotted onto the field, I found myself looking for Waymen's sister, Elizabeth.

Waymen came up beside me and knocked on my helmet. "Someone special is watching you," he said.

Was he reading my mind?

"Wh-who?" I said.

"A scout from Notre Dame University. And another from North Carolina. And one more from Oklahoma."

"Wh-what?!"

He grinned. "I can see no one has tried to recruit you yet. All three of them have been calling our house since early last year. Dad heard they're all interested in watching you play now too."

He banged my shoulder pads. "Just think. We could play on the same university team. Cool, huh?"

I grinned back. That would be cool. Having a friend sure beat not having one.

But for me to get to the same university with Waymen, I needed to play well.

Tonight we were up against the Cardwell Cardinals, one of two undefeated teams in the league. If we beat them, we would go to two and one, and so would they. Which meant if our record was still tied by the play-offs, we would have the advantage because we had beaten them.

Unfortunately, their offense was as good as ours.

For each of our touchdowns, they answered in return.

The game became a shootout.

They couldn't stop Whalin' Waymen Whitley. But we couldn't stop them either.

When the dust began to settle at the end of the fourth quarter, we were on the losing end of a 42–35 score. I had made twenty receptions and scored two touchdowns. That wouldn't matter, though, unless we won.

We got the ball on our five-yard line with less than three minutes left in the game.

Waymen faced us in the huddle. "John Elway," he said. "'Eighty-six. Against Cleveland in the AFC Championship. Down 20–13. Ninety-eight yards to go with less than two minutes in the game. And Denver won."

Waymen gave us his big grin. "Do you believe?"

"We believe!" we shouted.

"All right," Waymen said. "Coach wants us to run a crisscross with both outside slants coming back in. Got it?"

We got it.

And so did Waymen. He fired a pass up the middle as I stretched my hands over my shoulders. The ball grazed my fingertips and popped off the helmet of their cornerback. The ball popped up, then settled in my hands like I'd had a string attached to it.

I carried the ball ten more yards before both their safeties slammed me down.

Back in the huddle, Waymen grinned again. "Not often you see a quarterback play a pool shot like that, huh."

That was one of the good things about Waymen. He kept us loose. And as he promised, he took us down the field, just like Elway did against Cleveland in 'eighty-six.

The final play—with five seconds left in the game—was a quarterback sneak that Waymen took across the line untouched.

Now we were down only 42–41. All we needed was the extra point to tie the game.

The crowd screamed and cheered as Waymen took advantage of the break to trot over to the sidelines. When he came back, he met us in the huddle.

"Boys," he said, "I talked Coach into letting us go for the two-pointer. I mean, if we go into overtime, they get the ball. And they've been going through us like . . . um . . . food through a goose. I don't want to give them that chance. What do you say we beat them right now?"

"Yeah!" we all shouted back.

"We're gonna give them a play-action fake," Waymen said. He looked at the offensive linemen. "Think you can explode off the line like we're going to run the ball?"

He didn't wait for their answer. "I'm going to need two receivers in motion on the left side. And Linden, you trip and fall over the goal line."

I raised my eyebrows.

"See," he said, "I'll fake the hand-off. That should draw their cornerback at least a step toward me. If you fall, he'll relax. As you get up, angle toward the goalpost. Stop in front and spin toward me. The ball will be in your hands."

And that's how it went.

Our center snapped the ball. Waymen tucked it into the runningback's belly, then pulled it away. The runningback burst for the goal line as if he had the ball, drawing their tackles toward him. Waymen held the ball down at the side of his leg.

As I reached the goalpost—with no one on me—Waymen brought the ball up and fired it into my hands.

Two points! Putting us ahead 43–42! End of game!

It was sweet enough as a victory, but it got even better after I had showered and changed.

A man wearing a Notre Dame jacket was waiting outside the locker room for me. He was a short, skinny guy whose handlebar mustache curved under his big nose.

"Roy Linden?" he asked.

I nodded yes.

"You played a big game," he said. "Any chance I can make arrangements to talk to you and your folks sometime?"

Wow.

I wondered if I was dreaming.

Then, less than ten minutes after he had finished talking to me, I wondered if I was living a nightmare.

Nineteen

I had parked my truck in the corner of the parking lot. The light above it was out, and that put the truck in shadows.

That should have made me cautious. The light had not been out when I first parked.

I didn't think of that until it was too late. Until I'd gotten to my truck and someone stepped out of the shadows beside it.

He was a tall man with shoulders as wide as a cement truck. He wore a black jacket and a black ball cap that made his face impossible to see. I wished I had a flashlight.

"Boy," he said, "you and me is going to have a talk."

He spoke country, his voice a drawl that made the word *talk* sound like "taw-uk."

"And don't do anything stupid like try to run," he said. "I'd hate to have to get rough."

I looked hard. He was still in the shadow of the truck. His hands were out of sight. *Did he have a gun?*

He answered my unspoken question.

"I don't plan on getting rough with you," he said. "I ain't so stupid as to try anything here in the parking lot. Fact is, I don't even have Kentucky boxing gloves in my pocket."

Kentucky boxing gloves. I shivered at the thought. Some places in the hills, knife fights were so common that knives were known as boxing gloves.

"No sir," he said. "But your gramma, she lives alone. Isolated, if you get my drift."

"Y-y-you h-hurt h-her and I'll sp-spend my l-life h-hunting you d-down."

"I won't have to touch a hair on her head if you just git in the truck and sit and talk with me." He shook his head. "'Course, by the way you talk, it might take us till dawn."

He laughed. Not me. My hands were clenched so tight that my palms began to hurt where my nails were digging into them.

"Come on," he said, "I jest want to talk. If I was going to hurt you, I'd have found another place and used other ways. And believe me, I know 'em all."

As he walked to the passenger door, I got into the truck on my side. My eyes hit the tape recorder sitting on the center of the seat. The tape recorder I had used to report the black car was following me. I didn't want this man to see it.

I casually tossed my jacket over the tape recorder. Then I took a deep breath.

What now?

The passenger door was locked. All I had to do was lock my door, start the truck, and drive away.

But then Gram might get hurt. And no matter what I did to him after—because most surely I would hunt him down—it wouldn't make up for Gram getting hurt.

I looked over at the passenger side. He was waiting. I took so long to decide, he finally bent down to look at me.

I rolled down my window so I could shout for help if I needed to. Then I reached over and unlocked the other door. He slid onto the seat. The collar of his jacket was up and his cap was still pulled down low. I still couldn't see his face.

"You were thinking of leaving me behind, weren't you?" he asked.

My silence was answer enough.

"Good to see you were smart, boy. That should make this talk a lot easier."

"Wh-hat d-do you w-want?" It made me mad that my stutter made me sound afraid.

"I want you to stop messing around with this water thing. You just sit tight and listen while I spell things out."

Before I could answer, a voice rang across the parking lot.

"Hey, Roy!" It was Waymen, jogging toward the truck.

"Send him packing, boy," the man said. "Don't try anything dumb. You and me is just having a talk. You make me angry, and your gramma becomes fish bait."

Waymen reached the truck. He leaned on the door and looked in the window.

"Milk shake?" Waymen asked.

"G-good idea," I said. "I'll m-m-meet you."

Waymen reached over me to offer his hand to the man beside me.

"Hello, sir," Waymen said, "Waymen Whitley."

I took advantage of the moment to pull my jacket toward me. I dragged the tape recorder with it. With jacket and tape recorder pressed against my thigh, I slid my hand beneath the jacket.

"Yeah," the man said. "Great game."

He had turned just enough for me to get a quick look at his face. Long, thin nose. Pointy chin. And a missing front tooth. The same guy who had offered the money to Gram. So this *was* about the Johns Corporation.

"Thanks," Waymen said. "Gotta go. Roy, see you there, right?"

"R-right."

As Waymen's footsteps faded, the man began talking again.

"It's simple, boy. You can have it all, or you can lose it all."

I didn't understand.

"It's great isn't it," he said, "playing football with the famous Whalin' Waymen Whitley. You and him, you're such a good team, you got a shot at the state

93

championship. It's getting you noticed by university scouts. Once you get recruited, you'll get good coaching. Who knows, boy, maybe it'll get you a shot at the pros, and you can bring down a couple million a year. And all of it is getting started because of Whalin' Waymen. Without him, this team is nothing."

I still didn't understand.

"Think back, boy. When was it that Whalin' showed up? Wasn't it just after you took those jars of water to the county office?"

I thought. He was right.

"See, the people you're buckin' against, they ain't dumb. Soon's the health inspector recognized what was in the water and called them, they went out and hired Waymen's old man."

"Wh-hat w-was in the w-water?" I had my own guess. In the last few days, I had been doing some research. About industrial pollution. I'd discovered that some chemicals are hard to break down safely and are very expensive to treat. So unethical companies sometimes dump the chemicals illegally. And the illegal chemicals sometimes leaked, poisoning the environment. If the Johns Corporation was threatening me and Gram, we must have guessed right. There must be something in that mine shaft near Gram's water supply.

"You ain't listening to me, boy. They offered Waymen's old man so much money he was willing to move his family immediately. And they did it for one simple reason. You."

"M-me?"

"To make you happy, boy. Folks in this town know how good you are. For two years now, they been saying what a shame it is there weren't no quarterback good enough to make you shine. Now you got your quarterback. That is, *if* you behave."

What had Waymen said? His dad was getting triple his old salary? Could what this man was saying be true?

"Here's the other side of the coin, boy. If you don't behave, your gramma gets hurt. Waymen's old man gets fired. You lose your quarterback and your shot at getting scouted, not to mention the pros. In other words, drop what you're doing, and life will be just fine. Got it?"

"L-let me g-get this straight," I said a few seconds later. "The J-johns C-corporation is trying to h-hide s-something. If I l-let it d-drop—"

"I didn't say the Johns Corporation."

"You s-said whoever's b-behind this hired Waymen's f-father. Th-that's who he w-works for."

"Boy, right this moment you are doing precisely what I'm saying you should stop doing. Looking for answers. All I'm going to tell you is that you're a fool to go up against them. This is a backwoods county lost in the mountains. Nobody outside cares what happens here. The Johns Corporation owns this county and has for the last seventy years. Sheriff, newspaper, everybody. Don't mess with them. Got it?"

He didn't wait for my answer.

He opened the door and climbed out. After he slammed the door shut, he leaned down and looked at me through the window one final time.

"Just remember, boy. You can have it all or lose it all. Your gramma? I know where she sleeps. And I love any excuse to watch a good fire burn."

Then he was gone.

Twenty

Cat got your tongue?" Waymen asked me. "You haven't said a word since you got here."

We were in Al's Ice Cream Parlor. For the last ten minutes, kids and adults had walked past our table, slapping us on the back, telling us how great we'd played.

"A t-t-tiny, m-mean c-cat," I said, "k-keeps shaking my t-t-tongue and m-m-makes m-me t-talk funny."

Waymen grabbed his chest like he was having a heart attack. "What?! You made a joke!"

I couldn't help but grin. I *had* told a joke. Not only that, but I'd told one about my stuttering. Not that I'd tell Waymen, but he was great to hang with. He did what friends should do. Made me feel good.

I grabbed my chocolate milk shake and slurped hard, dropping my head so that Waymen couldn't see my eyes. I didn't want him to be able to read my thoughts.

Here I was, enjoying his friendship, and I had to make a decision that could get his dad fired. And I knew how much this new job meant to his family.

It seemed like it would be much easier just to listen to the guy in the black cap and drop this whole water thing. Then Gram wouldn't get hurt. And Waymen's family wouldn't get hurt. Not only that, I'd probably be able to go to college on a scholarship.

I felt rotten.

And Gram's words—about how much a person's soul was worth—kept haunting me.

She and I have talked a lot about things like that. Gram has no trouble understanding that people have souls to go along with their bodies and minds. She says something that's as invisible but as strong as love is good enough proof for her. Love is clearly something bigger than body and mind; it not only comes from the soul but also fills the soul. She says a lot of people try to fill their empty souls by chasing money or drugs or a whole lot of other things that leave them emptier than when they started. And all they need is love. She says once they understand they have souls, then they have to ask why, and what their souls were meant to do. Those were the questions that made life worth living no matter how tough the situation.

I slurped more of my milk shake, trying to think through my situation.

I knew I couldn't just quit on the water thing. It would bother me the rest of my life. No matter how much money I made thanks to a degree or pro football,

I would always know deep inside that I had gotten it the wrong way. And that would cost me my soul.

I lifted my eyes and looked at Waymen. He grinned back.

"W-would you ever t-t-take the easy w-w-way out if it m-meant doing the wr-wrong th-thing?"

He thought for a few moments, understanding the seriousness in my voice.

"I hope I wouldn't," he finally said. "Mom and Dad have always taught me that the Bible is something to live by—not just something to read on Sundays. But sometimes doing the right thing might be real hard. You asking for a reason?"

"M-maybe," I said.

"If you need help," he said, "whatever it is, I'll back you. All you need to do is say the word."

I had to look away. I knew he meant what he said. A guy couldn't ask for more in a friend.

"I n-need help," I said when I looked back at him.

"You got it," he said.

I was beginning to have an idea.

"L-let me t-tell you what's b-been happening," I said. "And l-let me t-tell you about our secret w-weapon."

 # *Twenty-One*

Because he wanted to help, Waymen joined me and Gram after dark the next night, high in the backwoods hills.

"Spooky," Waymen said. He shivered in his heavy sweater.

He was right, of course. It was a totally black night. Clouds had moved in, covering the tops of the hills with fog and blocking the moon and stars.

I had parked my truck at the end of a narrow dirt road. I'd left the engine running and the headlights on. The lights cut through wisps of fog, making it look like angels were slowly dancing around us.

Gram was in the truck, waiting in the warmth of the cab.

"S-spooky," I agreed. "J-j-ust be g-glad we're h-here with Gram's kin."

Waymen quickly nodded. I think he was still rattled from meeting the two cousins of Gram's long-dead husband.

They were hill people and not fond of having strangers in their midst. They were almost Gram's age and had stopped going to school after sixth grade. Which was not to say they were dumb. They just weren't schooled. They could track a squirrel across flat rock and read a man's thoughts by looking at his face. And they were tough. Real tough. The kind of tough that comes from working in a coal mine ten hours a day, six days a week, every week of the year.

And that's where they were right now.

Down a coal mine shaft. One that had not been mined for years.

After a half-hour of waiting, Waymen had gotten pretty edgy.

Owls hooted from the darkness beyond the truck's headlights. Trees cast shadows like deformed giants. And little animals rustled in the bushes. I had spent so many summers in these hills, for me, it was like enjoying a night out in my backyard.

"Did I tell you how angry my dad was when I told him about what they tried to do to you?" Waymen asked.

"About a d-dozen times," I said, grinning. "L-like m-maybe you n-need to h-hear your own v-voice."

"Maybe I do," he said. "I'm a city boy, remember."

A second later, an owl hooted.

"Did I say this is spooky?" he asked.

"F-four times."

"And what if someone from the Johns Corporation shows up? What if the guy in the black car followed us and—"

Two figures suddenly appeared in the headlights, walking toward us through the fog.

"Good guys, right?" Waymen said. "Please tell me they're the good guys."

"D-don't w-wet your pants," I said. "Th-they're c-coming from the m-mine."

"Maybe they got your gram's cousins and are coming to get us," he answered in a low voice. "I saw this movie once where the good guys turned out to be the bad guys. And we're twenty miles from the nearest town . . ."

As they got closer, I saw that one man held a video camera in one hand and a jar in the other. The jar sloshed with a clear liquid.

"G-good g-guys," I said. "W-with g-good news."

"Roy," the first man called out as he moved far enough into the light for us to see his bearded face. He was Gram's cousin Stewart. "You wuz right. There wuz hundreds of barrels down at the bottom. A bunch leaked all over. You could see stains where something got on the floor of the shaft."

"I cain't read much," Clem, the other cousin, said. Not only did both have long beards streaked with gray, both also wore greasy ball caps, dark flannel shirts, and denim overalls. "But I can cipher enough to git by. I done scratched down on a piece of paper the name on the barrels."

He held up the jar. "And I got some of it from a barrel what hadn't spilled."

"Y-you d-didn't touch the s-s-stuff," I said.

"No sirree," he said as he showed me his gloves. "From what you told us earlier, I'd just as soon grab a rattlesnake."

He handed me the jar and the video camera. "You'd be right proud of me, Roy," Clem said. "I was able to point and shoot just like you showed me. Stewart lit it all good with his flashlight, and it weren't no problem putting all them barrels into this here camera. 'Course, there's a couple places where Stewart's doing a little jig dance, just cause he ain't ever been on television."

"Hope you don't mind," Stewart said, looking down and scuffing his foot. Old as he was, the shyness made him almost cute, in spite of the shotgun he carried.

"Y-you g-g-ot everything we n-needed," I said. "Th-thanks."

"'T'weren't nothing," Clem said. "The both of you, just keep making us proud with your football playing."

"Yes, sir," Waymen said.

There was one last thing I had to ask Stewart and Clem.

"W-would it be all right if G-gram stayed with you for a f-few d-days?" I said. I told them about the weasel-faced man. "N-no s-sense taking ch-chances."

"Be a pleasure," Clem said. "If that feller in the black car shows up looking for trouble, he'll get plenty."

 *Twenty-Two*

I had felt at home wearing blue jeans and a sweater, waiting in the woods late at night.

But the next afternoon, I did not feel at home in a suit and tie, waiting in a plush room deep in the Johns Corporation building.

I looked around the conference room where presentations were made to employees. At one end of the room a television sat on a stand, hooked up to a VCR. A large oval table filled the center of the room. Rolling chairs with deep cushions lined the table. On the walls, there were large oil paintings of ships at sea. The thick carpet made the room feel hushed.

The only thing that calmed my nerves was the fact that Waymen and his dad were beside me.

Mr. Whitley was as tall and lean as Waymen. You could tell by their faces they were father and son. Mr. Whitley's hair, though thinner and shorter than Waymen's, was the same color. Laugh lines etched the corners of Mr. Whitley's mouth and eyes, showing what Waymen would look like in twenty years. They, too, wore dark suits.

"I'm n-n-nervous," I told Waymen as I shifted my weight from one foot to the other and back again. "Wh-hat if h-he shows up with l-lawyers or s-something."

"Relax, country boy," Waymen said. "Besides, I've seen you on the football field. You could outrun any army he brings."

We had been waiting fifteen minutes. I would have been happier in a spooky fog at the end of a dirt road. We were waiting for the president of the Johns Corporation. I had only seen him in photos in the newspapers, generally when he'd written a check to some local charity. Not that writing checks hurt him. He had millions of dollars. Not only that, his family had also controlled this county for years and years, long before I had been born. What was I doing here?

"D-did I t-tell you how mad Gram was wh-when I m-made her s-stay with her c-c-cousins?"

Waymen grinned. "About a dozen times. Like maybe you need to hear the sound of your own voice."

"V-v-very f-funny," I said.

Before Waymen could say anything else, the door opened.

Albert Wayne Johns III walked into the room. Alone.

I recognized him from the newspaper photos, but I had expected him to be bigger. He had surprisingly narrow shoulders. He wore a perfectly pressed suit, with his hair slicked back to complete the tailored look. His gold-rimmed glasses reflected light as he entered, and he smelled faintly of aftershave.

"Good afternoon," he said, stepping close. "Mr. Whitley, I've heard a lot about your son and his leadership on the football team. I'm pleased to finally meet him."

He shook Waymen's hand.

"And you, of course, are Roy Linden," he said, taking my hand. His skin was soft, his grip light. "Star receiver."

After shaking Mr. Whitley's hand, he asked us to sit down. Then he asked us why we had requested this meeting.

Mr. Whitley and Waymen both looked at me.

Just like my conversation with Eldon Mawther at the newspaper, I had written and practiced a script of what I wanted to say.

I began, feeling this was as unreal as the movie I was trying to pretend it was.

"We are here, sir," I said, repeating my memorized script, "because we want you to know that someone in your organization is dumping chemicals down an old mine shaft."

Mr. Whitley had helped Waymen and me figure out how to approach Mr. Johns. If he didn't know about the chemicals—if he was innocent—he would want to know. And then he would help stop the dumping and clean up the leaking chemicals himself.

On the other hand, if he knew about it . . .

Mr. Johns gave me a puzzled frown. He was either surprised, or—if he was guilty of something—curious about how much we knew.

I continued. I told him the story from the beginning, just as I had memorized it. The dead birds, the health inspector, the newspaper reporter, my tests in the school science lab. I got through all of the first part without stuttering.

Not once did he try to stop me. He just watched me, as if I were an interesting insect he'd trapped in a glass jar.

I took a breath and waited to see if he had any questions. He did.

"Very interesting," he said. "This is a serious charge. Do you have any proof?"

Was he an innocent man worried that someone in his company had dumped chemicals illegally? Or a guilty man worried that he had been caught?

I nodded at Waymen. He stood.

"If you don't mind, sir." Waymen walked to the television and popped a videotape into the VCR.

He turned on the television. It hissed loudly until Waymen adjusted the volume. Gray and white specks danced across the screen. Then images appeared. Images of barrels lit by a flashlight beam.

The images jerked around the screen as Gram's cousin Clem walked closer to the barrels with the video camera.

We heard his voice. "The boy was telling the truth, Stewart. Wonder what this stuff is?"

Stewart stepped in front of the camera and did a little dance.

"Stewart!" Clem said. "Quit that fooling around!"

"Shucks," Stewart said, "Don't I look purty?"

The video camera showed a different angle as Clem shot it at Stewart's feet. It was easy to see where stuff had leaked from the barrels and seeped into the ground. There were also tire tracks, probably from a forklift.

Finally, the camera zoomed in on the letters stenciled across the barrels.

POLYCHLORINATED BIPHENYLS. Otherwise known as PCBs. I'd done some more research after Gram's cousins made this tape. PCBs were used in the making of electrical appliances. I'd discovered that years ago they were dumped into the upper Hudson River in New York. Commercial fishing is still restricted in some areas. Once this stuff gets into the environmental chain, the toxic chemical builds up in all species.

There was one more shot of Stewart dancing. Then the camera shut off.

"Amusing as the dancing hillbilly was, I'm not sure this is much proof," Albert Wayne Johns III said. "That footage could have been shot anywhere."

"The men who made that tape are willing to testify that those barrels are in an abandoned mine shaft that belongs to the Johns Corporation," Waymen said. "We also have a sample taken from one of the barrels. Isn't that proof enough?"

"Not proof that anyone from the Johns Corporation

put those barrels there," Mr. Johns said. "We'll dispose of them immediately. But without taking any blame."

"No, sir," Mr. Whitley said. Mr. Whitley set his hands down on the table. I could see his knuckles, scarred from years of working honestly with his hands. "That will not do at all. From what I understand, it costs a lot of money to dispose of these chemicals properly. I'm willing to bet that someone has made a small fortune by agreeing to dispose of them and instead hiding them in the mine shaft. Not only should the chemicals be cleaned up, but the person responsible should also be found and punished."

Albert Wayne Johns III arched an eyebrow. Although he kept his voice quiet, I could tell he was really mad. Maybe that's how it was with people with money. They thought others should listen to their whispers as if they were shouting. "I do not expect to be spoken to in that tone of voice. Not from a mere employee. And especially not from one who is here through my generosity."

"Your generosity?" Mr. Whitley asked. His fingers flexed into fists on the table.

Mr. Johns did not notice. He continued. "Why would I bring *you* into my company at the salary you now receive? I simply wanted your son to play on our high school's football team. I knew if I made it worth your while, you'd move—immediately."

Mr. Johns smiled a nasty smile. "You now receive triple what you're worth. Can you really afford to lose this job?"

Mr. Johns turned to me. "And do you want to lose your chance at a scholarship?"

I said nothing.

"As I thought," Mr. Johns said. "Well, just leave me the videotape and let me handle this problem."

He stood up. "Now, please. I'm a busy man. We'll say good-bye and pretend none of this happened."

"N-not so f-fast," I said. "Y-you w-won't get away th-this easily."

Mr. Johns didn't know it, but this had been a fishing trip. And we had just landed the big one.

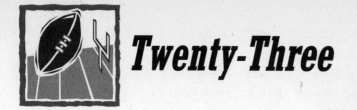

Twenty-Three

N-not s-so f-ast?" Mr. Johns said, mocking my stutter. "Are you stupid?"

"Dumb move, Mr. Fancy Suit," Waymen said. "People who make fun of Roy usually regret it."

"This is great," Mr. Johns said. "I'm looking at a mechanic and his football jock of a son and a kid who stutters like a baby. Why should I be afraid of any of you?"

I had run out of memorized script to work with. But I didn't care.

"Th-this," I said. I pulled my mini-recorder from my inside suit pocket. It was the secret weapon that had given me the idea of facing Mr. Johns.

"Hah," Mr. Johns said. "I haven't said a single word that could get me in trouble in court. How childish, taping this conversation."

"N-not th-this conversation," I said. "An earlier one—w-with someone who works for y-you."

I pushed the play button. Words came out clearly. Words said in the front seat of my truck a few nights earlier.

See, the people you're buckin' against, they ain't dumb. Soon's the health inspector recognized what was in the water and called them, they went out and hired Waymen's old man . . .

Mr. Johns's smile faded fast.

You ain't listening to me, boy. They offered Waymen's old man so much money he was willing to move his family immediately. And they did it for one simple reason. You. . . .

In the pickup truck, when the man in the black cap had slipped inside, I'd thrown my jacket over the tape recorder.

To make you happy, boy. Folks in this town know how good you are. For two years now, they been saying what a shame it is there weren't no quarterback good enough to make you shine. Now you got your quarterback. That is, if you behave. . . .

Waymen had come up to the truck to invite me for a milk shake. It had given me a chance to hit the record button on the tape recorder.

Here's the other side of the coin, boy. If you don't behave, your gramma gets hurt. Waymen's old man gets fired. You lose your quarterback and your shot at getting scouted, not to mention the pros. In other words, drop what you're doing, and life will be just fine. Got it? . . .

By itself, the conversation on tape might not have been enough to get Mr. Johns in trouble. But Mr.

Johns had just made the same threat. That tied them together.

Boy, right this moment you are doing precisely what I'm saying you should stop doing. Looking for answers. All I'm going to tell you is that you're a fool to go up against them. This is a backwoods county lost in the mountains. Nobody outside cares what happens here. The Johns Corporation owns this county and has for the last seventy years. Sheriff, newspaper, everybody. Don't mess with them. Got it?

"Give me that!" Mr. Johns snarled. He swept his arm toward me. So quickly I hardly saw it happen, Mr. Whitley stood and grabbed the man's fist.

"I was hoping you weren't behind this," Mr. Whitley said. He held Mr. Johns's fist and squeezed with a powerful hand. "But with everything else and with what you've said over the last ten minutes, I think there's enough for the authorities to begin an investigation. They'll trace your bank accounts to see if you've deposited money that you can't explain from regular business. They'll check your spending habits to see if you've been spending more than you make legitimately. You know they'll find that money, and they'll trace it backward to find out who has been paying you to dump the toxic chemicals. Yes sir, they'll put together whatever extra proof they need to get you a nice long jail sentence."

"Nice try," Mr. Johns said. He tried to pull his hand away. Mr. Whitley just kept holding it. "But I own this town. No one will lift a finger against me."

"Maybe. But you don't own the FBI," Mr. Whitley said.

"The FBI?" Mr. Johns said. "Don't be ridiculous."

"I'm not being ridiculous. How do you think I know so much about what they'll do?"

"You're bluffing," Mr. Johns said. But he didn't sound certain.

"Waymen?" Mr. Whitley said.

Waymen pulled off his suit coat. He unbuttoned the front of his shirt. His bare chest showed what the FBI had taped in place earlier. A transmitter. Waymen was wired, just like an undercover cop.

"You see," Mr. Whitley said. "The FBI is already involved in this. They came down from Lexington when I called them this morning and told them what we had. The video, the chemical samples, the recording. And even an offer on Mrs. Linden's land and cabin from the Johns Corporation. They found it all very interesting. They were kind enough to rig Waymen with this fancy recording gear. They're outside in a van and have heard every word you said."

Mr. Whitley finally dropped Mr. Johns's fist.

"The FBI," Mr. Johns repeated. He rubbed his hand. His voice was the voice of a man suddenly very afraid.

"The FBI," Mr. Whitley answered. "They want to know all about the chemicals. And about how you manipulate this town. If my guess is right, they should be knocking on the door in a couple of minutes."

Mr. Whitley was wrong. It only took thirty seconds.

Twenty-Four

This is what is exciting and sad and fun and mysterious and scary about life: The end of something is always the beginning of something else.

Like with Albert Wayne Johns III. After the FBI investigated, he was charged and found guilty of breaking the Toxic Substances Control Act and the Resource Conservation and Recovery Act. They also got him for fraud, bribery, and—worst of all—tax evasion charges for not reporting his illegal income. My name made the papers. So did Whalin' Waymen Whitley's.

That should have been the end of it.

But there is something else wonderful and frightening about life: It will push you to grow as much as you let it.

What do I mean? It's easy to sit at home and watch television—you don't have to take any chances that way. But if you are willing to make mistakes and try new things, you'll discover you can do a lot more than you ever dreamed.

The end of Albert Wayne Johns III brought a new beginning for me because my investigation and my friendship with Waymen had nudged me out of my little box—as if God, like a mother bird, had gently pushed me out of the nest. Baby birds don't know when they're ready to fly, but their mothers do. For those baby birds in the first few moments as they learn to use their wings, life must feel exciting and sad and fun and mysterious and scary.

And so—on a Saturday night three months after football season ended—I stood behind a curtain on a stage in front of five hundred people. Wearing pajamas. With my heart revved up like a race car engine as I waited for a girl to scream.

"Aaaaaaaaah!" Elizabeth Whitley shouted at the top of her lungs. Only she wasn't Elizabeth Whitley. She was the maid in a murder mystery who had just discovered a dead body.

"Aaaaaaaaah!"

I strolled onto the stage, glad that I could keep my legs moving. I was afraid if I stood still while I spoke, my legs would shake so much that I would fall over. That wouldn't be good. Not during my first moment ever as an actor.

"Miss Marie," I said. I walked carefully along the exact lines on the stage floor that our drama coach had practiced with us again and again. "How many times have I told you not to disturb my sleep."

"But Mr. Rich," she said. "Look! It's your brother! He's dead!"

She pointed at a bed on the stage. A pair of feet stuck out from beneath the bed.

"Hmm . . . interesting," I said. I paused. The silence was heavy. I knew five hundred pairs of eyes were on me. But in that moment, I felt great. I had practiced for weeks for this moment, and I wasn't stuttering. "Miss Marie, have you looked beneath the bed to see the man's face?"

"No," she answered. "I just this moment found the body."

"Interesting," I repeated. "Then how do you know it is my brother? Or that he is even dead? From here, only the feet are visible."

She opened her eyes wide and stared straight at me. "The shoes," she said. "I know they are his shoes."

I paced back and forth several times. Then I grabbed her shoulder and spun her toward me. "Tell me," I said. "How do you know they are his shoes?"

She raised her left hand to her mouth and bit the knuckle of her forefinger. Then she fled from the stage.

I moved to a desk beside the bed. I picked up the telephone receiver and dialed a number.

"Yes," I said a few seconds later. "Martha? It's Joshua Rich here. It looks like our little plan is working."

And the play was off and running. . . .

An hour and a half later, I stood with five other actors to take our bows as the crowd gave us a standing ovation.

It actually felt better than the last five minutes of the final football game of the season when everyone knew we were about to win the state championship.

It even felt better than the scholarship offer I had accepted at Notre Dame. The same university where Waymen was headed next year. The end of Albert Wayne Johns III had helped me realize that I was interested in investigative journalism. I looked forward to starting on a degree.

Why did I feel so good as the applause rolled over us? Not because I had cured my stutter. I hadn't. Although it was getting better, off the stage I still struggled. Not as much as before. But it was still there.

No, as the applause kept going, I realized I felt so good for one simple reason.

I had found my wings.

An Excerpt from

Titan Clash

Book Four in the Sports Mystery Series

I couldn't tell whether the crowd in the gymnasium was more excited about the basketball game or the chance to win a free pickup truck.

Turner, Indiana, is definitely crazy about high school basketball. Our town has 1,954 people. And on this Saturday afternoon, 1,952 of them had turned out to watch the season-opening game of the Turner High Titans. The only two people missing were the Gould brothers, in jail for unpaid speeding tickets. Plus there were another 600 fans for the Wolford Wolves, a high school fifteen miles away.

As if that weren't enough, the high school band, the entire cheerleading team, and television and radio crews added to the chaos, along with 150 white pigeons.

Yes, 150 pigeons, on stage, in a large cage, in front of the band. They were about to be released as part of a promotion for Turner Chev-Olds, the local car dealership where my dad worked as head accountant.

Dad stood beside the pigeon cage, with a man named Ike Bothwell who owned Turner Chev-Olds. He held a microphone, waiting for the music to end. Dad and Ike had been best friends since high school.

Dad wore what he always did—white shirt, black pants, black suspenders, and a red bow tie.

Ike's checkered-shirt, blue jeans, and cowboy boots were the trademark clothes he wore during his late-night television commercials, where he told folks to "come on down to Turner Chev-Olds for the best old-fashioned deals in the state." Not many people had been "coming on down" lately, though, and that was the reason for the pigeons.

Ike grinned and tapped his feet to the music.

Dad just frowned with his arms crossed. Dad didn't like the pigeon-promotion idea or anything fun.

Ike did. He had thought up the idea.

One of the pigeons had a capsule tied to its leg with a tiny strip of paper. Inside the capsule was a coupon to win a brand-new pickup truck. When the paper tore, as all paper does eventually, the capsule would fall from the pigeon's leg. If someone found that capsule, they'd get the truck.

That was the key word: *If.*

Two days earlier, when we'd talked about the pigeons, Ike had laughed a big belly laugh and told me that there was very little chance anyone would find the capsule. It could end up anywhere in the county. The whole point, Ike had said, was the free publicity the car dealership would get.

By the looks of the crowd in the gym, it was working.

Everything was set except the release of the pigeons. Then the basketball game would begin, which was all I really cared about.

The rest of the guys on the Titans felt the same way. I could see they were restless.

My eyes caught those of the Titan's newest player, Chuck Murray. He gave me a wink and a grin, as if he knew I just wanted to get to the game. And that he wanted to as well.

I winked back. On the stage, the music stopped.

Ike tapped the microphone. It squealed out some noise.

"Folks!" he shouted. It was so loud that several people winced. "It's the kickoff of our biggest sales event of the year! Come on down to Turner Chev-Olds for the best old-fashioned deals! Zero down and a couple hundred a month gets you a brand-new car!"

"Just let them go, Ike!" someone shouted.

"Yeah, Ike!" someone else shouted. "I want that free truck!"

So did everyone else in town. Including my best friend, Tom Sawyer. Yes. Tom Sawyer like the character in Mark Twain's book. People bug him about his name all the time.

I was worried about Tom. This morning, he had told me he had a plan to win the free truck. I hadn't seen Tom anywhere in the gym. I was half afraid he was waiting outside with a shotgun, ready to shoot the pigeons as they flew through the double doors.

"Folks!" Ike Bothwell shouted again into the squealing mike. "You ask, and Turner Chev-Olds delivers. Will someone at the back open the gym doors?"

The school janitor pushed them open.

Ike looked over at the high school band. The drummer nodded and made a long, theatrical drumroll.

Ike bowed, turned, and opened the cage door.

Nothing happened. The white pigeons stayed inside.

Ike looked at the 2500 people watching him and grinned stupidly. He shrugged and walked around to the back of the cage. He waved his arms, trying to shoo them out. Ike took off his hat and waved it. Finally, Ike kicked at the back of the cage. It began to fall forward.

He yelped and hooked his fingers around the bars of the cage but the cage just pulled him down with it.

It fell, cage door down, with a loud bang. The pigeons inside began to flap around, but they were trapped. Feathers flew everywhere, but the pigeons had no place to go.

Dad rolled his eyes, the way he always did with me when I said something he didn't find funny. Then he lif ed Ike away from the cage and turned the cage upright.

This time, those pigeons made a beeline out of the cage. In a whirring explosion of white, they burst into the gym and toward the open doors.

And, just as suddenly as the pigeons had exploded from the cage, my friend Tom Sawyer stepped into the doorway, armed with a giant butterfly net.